"You don't really think I'm going to walk out of my son's life?" he asked.

She was afraid again. "Please, Cal. You couldn't be so cruel as to try to take Robbie from me. I adore him. He's my son."

"He's my son too." Cal rose to his feet, standing over her. "Tonight I claim him. I have every intention of taking him back to Coronation Hill. He's a McKendrick. Coronation Hill is his home. It's his heritage. He's my heir."

Gina rose as well, anger and fear boiling in her great, dark eyes. "Just when do you think you could take him? Go on, tell me that. And what about me? Do you really think I'm going to stand around letting you do it? You'd have to kill me first."

His expression, unlike hers, couldn't have been cooler. He took hold of her wrist, letting her feel just a touch of his vastly superior strength. "No need to kill you, Gina," he drawled. "Marrying suits me better."

Welcome to the intensely emotional world of

MARGARET WAY

where rugged, brooding bachelors
meet their match in the burning heart
of Australia....

**A small selection of praise for some of
Margaret's best-loved Outback stories!**

"*Master of Maramba* by Margaret Way
is a fantastic tale with great character development
and charming scenes."
—*Romantic Times BOOKreviews*

"Margaret Way's *Outback Fire* is a pleasing story
with fiery characters and a strong premise."
—*Romantic Times BOOKreviews*

"Margaret Way's *Outback Surrender* is a page-turner.
The characters are so real and compelling
that you can't help being drawn into their lives
and rooting for them to overcome the obstacles
that have been put in their way."
—*Romantic Times BOOKreviews*

MARGARET WAY

Cattle Rancher, Secret Son

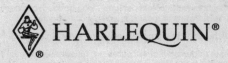

TORONTO • NEW YORK • LONDON
AMSTERDAM • PARIS • SYDNEY • HAMBURG
STOCKHOLM • ATHENS • TOKYO • MILAN • MADRID
PRAGUE • WARSAW • BUDAPEST • AUCKLAND

ISBN-13: 978-0-373-17493-5
ISBN-10:   0-373-17493-4

CATTLE RANCHER, SECRET SON

First North American Publication 2008.

www.eHarlequin.com

Printed in U.S.A.

Margaret Way takes great pleasure in her work and works hard at her pleasure. She enjoys tearing off to the beach with her family at weekends, loves haunting galleries and auctions and is completely given over to French champagne "for every possible joyous occasion." She was born and educated in the river city of Brisbane, Australia, and now lives within sight and sound of beautiful Moreton Bay.

Journey to the Outback
with Margaret Way's fabulous new duet,
only from Harlequin Romance®.

Coming in September and October

PROLOGUE

FATE, Destiny, Chance: call it what you will, it has a hand in everything.

Gina Romano, a young woman of twenty-four, whose classical bone structure, golden skin, lustrous dark eyes and hair richly proclaimed her Italian heritage, was walking to her friend Tanya's front gate. It had been a lovely relaxing afternoon with Tanya and her beautiful new baby, Lily-Anne.

Tanya, cradling tiny Lily-Anne, naturally the most beautiful baby in the world, was standing at the front door, waving Gina off: Gina's hand was on the wrought-iron gate making sure it was closed securely after her, when she felt a tingle like an icy finger on her nape. It alerted her, bringing on a familiar feeling of alarm. Every time she felt that icy finger, and she had felt it many times in her life, she took it as a signal *something* was about to happen.

She pulled away from the gate, moving swiftly out onto the pavement, hands shaking, legs shaking, head humming as if it were filled with high tension wires. She was no clairvoyant but she had come to accept she had an extra sense most people either didn't have or didn't get to develop. It was a gift, simultaneously a curse; an inheritance handed down through the maternal line of her family as other families claimed the second sight.

The *noise* came first. One minute the leafy suburban street was drowsing under a turquoise sky, the next, a range of things happened. An early model car with its engine roaring and trailing grey-black clouds of exhaust fumes turned into the street without slowing at the corner. Gina watched the driver correct the skid, only to gun the engine even though the left front wheel was wobbling. Gina estimated he was doing a good fifteen to twenty kilometres over the fifty kilometre speed limit.

From the property directly opposite, the real estate agent overseeing the forthcoming auction, camera in hand, strode out onto the pavement on the way to his car. He stopped, took in the situation and cried out. Simultaneously a flame-haired cherub called Cameron from the house next door to Tanya's came bounding down his unfenced driveway and ran pell-mell onto the street without so much as a glance in either direction. He was totally oblivious to danger, his mind was set solely on retrieving his blue beach ball, which was fast bouncing away from him into the opposite gutter.

The estate agent, a man of sixty, to his everlasting horror was assailed by such a terrible feeling of helplessness he simply *froze,* but Gina, who didn't even hear Tanya yelling frantically so focused was she on the child, reacted like an Olympic sprinter coming off the blocks. Adrenaline poured into her body, causing a surge of power. She *flew* after the little boy, at one point her long legs fully extended front and back as she rose in an extravagant leap. Or so it appeared to the neighbours alerted by Tanya's screaming and the awful din set up by the smoking bomb. As one of them later confided to the television reporter, "It was the coolest thing I've ever seen. The young lady was moving so *impossibly* fast she was all but airborne. Ought to make the headlines!"

So this then was much more than a simple good deed. It was seen to be on the heroic scale. But Gina herself felt no sense of valour. She did what she thought anyone would have done in the circumstances. A child's life was on the line. What option did she have but to attempt to save it? Her very humanity demanded she act and act *fast*.

Heart almost bursting through her rib cage, she scooped up the child in the bare nick of time, her body sparkly all over as though wired, and then flew on to the safety of the grassy verge thinking there was no way she could avoid taking an awful fall or being pulverized by Tanya's formidable brick and wrought-iron fence. She had a vision of herself lying on the grass, moaning because of broken bones, maybe even covered in blood. But for now, her main thought was how to cushion the child whose vulnerable little head was buried against her breast.

Please, God...please, God! Every atom in her body braced in case He didn't hear her.

She needn't have worried. It had been decided all would be well. What could so easily have been a tragedy—glittering metal pulverising two tender bodies—turned into a feel-good human-interest story. A workman built like a double-door refrigerator but as light on his feet as a ballet dancer in his prime appeared out of nowhere to gather Gina and child in like it was a set piece of choreography. Little Cameron, now the drama was over, broke into frightened howls of *"Mum-eee! Mum-eee! Mum-eee!"* the *ees* mounting ever higher.

A distraught young woman, with orange locks that refused to lie down, was running to him, calling repeatedly, "My darling, my darling, my baby!" Gina, her own body trembling in after-shock handed Cameron over to his mother to an outpouring of thanks. Cameron, for some reason common to children, stopped his heart-wrenching wailing and began to laugh merrily. He reached into the pocket of his little blue shorts to hand Gina a couple of jelly beans he hadn't touched, presumably as a reward.

Incredibly it was all over in a matter of seconds, only now

there was a small crowd surrounding them who burst into spontaneous applause as though they had witnessed a great piece of stunt work. The battered car, scruffy young man at the wheel, didn't stop or even slow though he did flash a nonchalant hand out of the open window, obviously taking the philosophical view "all's well that ends well."

Angry fists were raised in his direction, cries of condemnation. A silver-haired old lady added a few words one would have thought she wouldn't even know, much less use, but he accelerated away, apparently with a clear conscience, mobile now glued to his ear. He would later be picked up by the police who were delighted to have his licence number handed to them on a plate. There was also the matter of a stack of parking fines he had completely ignored.

Praise shifted to the real estate agent. Belatedly, he had done something right. Momentarily transfixed by horror he might have been, but he had immediately swung into action on witnessing Gina's spectacular transformation into "Wonder Woman you'd have to call her! Used to love that show!" He was ready for a laugh now. Hadn't he snapped out of his sick panic to get "the whole blessed thing" on film?

Thus it was, Gina Romano found herself an unwilling heroine and would remain so for some time. Cameron's immensely grateful parents later went on television to say they would never forget what Ms Romano had done. In fact, viewers got the decided impression Gina was now part of the family. Tanya took the welcome opportunity to show off her beautiful baby to the larger world, added her own little bit. "Gina's so brave! Why only a few months back she saved Cameron from a big black dog."

"Let's hope there won't be a *third* time for wee Cameron!" the woman reporter joshed, smiling brilliantly into the camera.

Gina, the heroine of all this, prayed inwardly: *Don't let anyone recognise me.*

But recognised she was. By her colleagues and friends, just about everyone who knew her at her local shopping centre, the inhabitants of the small North Queensland sugar town a thousand miles away where she had been born and raised, and most crucially by the last person on earth she wanted to see her captured image; the man she had fallen hopelessly, madly, irrevocably in love with four years before. The man Fate had denied her. The man she had so carefully hidden herself away from. Not even her closest friends even suspected she knew him. Or *had* known him. *Intimately.*

Gina never discussed her former life, her secrets and her haunted past. She had a good life now for which she was very grateful. It had all the trappings of normality. She had an attractive apartment in a safe area with importantly a lovely little park nearby with a kiddies' play area. She had a well-paid job with a stockbroking firm who valued her services. She had men friends who admired and desired her. At least two of them definitely had marriage on their minds if mentioning it meant anything. Men, generally speaking, had to be helped along in these matters.

She couldn't commit. And she knew why. Hardly a day went by that she didn't think of the man who had taken her: body, mind and soul. Trying to forget him hadn't just been one long struggle: It was a battle she had come to accept she was doomed to lose.

CHAPTER ONE

Coronation Hill Station
The Northern Territory

FROM the crest of Crown Ridge, tumbled with smooth, near perfectly round boulders like a giant's marbles, Cal sat his magnificent silver-grey stallion, watching a section of the lowing herd being driven towards the holding yards at Yering Springs. From this incomparable vantage point on top of the ancient sandstone escarpment, the whole of Jabiru Valley was revealed to him. Silver billabongs lined by willowy melaleucas and groves of pandanus wound away to the left and right, the sun flashing off surfaces as smooth as glass. He could see the flocks of magpie geese and whistling ducks congregated around the banks and exploding from the reed beds. Wildlife was abundant in the Valley: native mammals, reptiles, trillions of insects and above all, the *birds*. The gloriously coloured parrots, the cockatoos, galahs, rosellas and lorikeets, countless other species, the beautiful water birds and, at the top of the chain, the reigning jabiru. It was the great numbers of jabirus, the country's only stork, fishing the billabongs and lagoons that had given the Valley its name.

The Territory was still a wild paradise with a mystical feel about it that he firmly believed derived from the aboriginal culture. The *Dreaming*. The spirit ancestors had fashioned this ancient land, creating everything in it. Where he now sat on his horse had provided natural art galleries in its numerous caves and rock shelters. Many of the walls were covered in ancient rock paintings, art treasures fiercely protected by the indigenous people and generations of McKendricks who had taken over the land.

In whatever direction he looked, the landscape was potent with beauty. He supposed he would have made a good pagan with his nature worship. Certainly he was very much in touch with the natural world. He even knew, like the aboriginals on the station, the places where great *energy* resided, certain sandstone monuments, special caves, rock pools and particular trees. The lily-covered lagoons on Coronation Hill were filled with magnificent waterlilies of many colours: pink, red, white, yellow, cream. His favourite was the sacred Blue Lotus. Underneath those gorgeous carpets it had to be mentioned, glided the odd man-eating croc or two. They had learned to take crocs in their stride. Crocodiles were a fact of life in the Territory. Don't bother them. They won't bother you.

God it was hot! He could feel trickles of sweat run down his nape and onto his back. He lifted a hand to angle his wide brimmed Akubra lower on his head, thinking his hair was getting much too long. It was curling up at the back like a girl's. He would have to get it cut when he found time. The mob had been on the move since the relative cool of dawn but now the heat was intense. The world of sky above him was stunningly clear of clouds, an infinity of burning blue. He loved his home with a passion. He loved the colours of the land. They weren't the furnace-reds of the Centre's deserts but cool blues and silvers, the deeper cobalts and amethysts. Instead of the rolling red sand dunes of the central part of the Territory, in the tropical north, the entire landscape was covered in every conceivable shade of lustrous green.

And flowers! Extraordinary flowers abounded in the Valley. The grevilleas, the banksias, the hakeas, the native hibiscus and the gardenias everyone knew, but there were countless other species unique to the far-away regions that had never been named. No one had ever had the time to get around to it. Australia was a dry, dry continent but oddly produced the most marvellous wildflowers that were becoming world renowned. Everywhere he looked exquisite flowers unfurled themselves on trees and shrubs, others rode the waving tops of the savannah grasses that could grow after the Wet a good four feet over his head and he was six feet two.

It was here in the mid-1860s, that his ancestor, the Scot, Alexander Campbell-McKendrick swore an oath to found his own dynasty in the savage wilderness of the Australian Outback. It was quite an ambition and a far, far, cry from his own ancestral home in the Borders region of Scotland. But as it stood, a second son, denied inheritance of the family estates by the existence of an elder brother, Alexander McKendrick, an adventurer and a visionary at heart, found an excellent option in travelling halfway across the world to seek his own fortune in the Great South Land, where handsome, well-educated young Scotsmen from distinguished families were thin on the ground. McKendrick had been very favourably received, immediately gaining the patronage of the Governor of the then self-governing colony of New South Wales.

The great quest had begun.

It had started in the colony of New South Wales, but was to finish far away in the Northern Territory, the wildest of wild frontiers, where a man could preside over a cattle run bigger than many a European country. This was the mysterious Top End of the great continent, deeply hostile country, peopled with a nation collectively called the *Kakadu*.

McKendrick had been undaunted. It was from this very escarpment he had named on the spot Crown Ridge because of its curious resemblance to an ancient crown. He had looked out over a limitless lushly grassed valley and he had recorded as "knowing in his heart" this was the place where the Australian dynasty of the Campbell-McKendrick family would put down roots. Land was the meaning of life. The land endured when mighty monuments and buildings collapsed and dissolved into dust.

So that was my great-great-great-great-grandfather, Cal thought with the familiar thrill of pride. *Some guy! And there is* my *inheritance spread out before me.* The McKendricks—they had abandoned their double barrel name by the turn of the twentieth century—were among the great pioneers of the Interior.

By late afternoon he was back at the homestead, dog-tired, bones aching after a long, hard day in the saddle. It was truly amazing the amount of punishment a young man's body could take. His father, Ewan, so recently a dynamo had slowed down considerably this past year. Ewan McKendrick was a legendary cattleman like the McKendricks before him. There had only been one black sheep in the family, the third heir, Duncan, the supposed *quiet* one, whose exploits when he came to power got him killed by an unerring aboriginal spear, the terrible consequence of ill-treating the black people on the station. It was a crime no McKendrick had committed before him and none ever did again.

Cal found his mother and father and his widower uncle Edward, his father's brother, in the library enjoying a gin and tonic and talking horses, a never-ending topic of conversation in the family. Their faces lit up at his arrival as if he had just returned from an arduous trek to the South Pole.

"Ah, there you are, darling," cried his mother, Jocelyn, extending an arm.

He went to her and put his hands lightly on her thin shoulders. A beautiful woman was his mother. She had made a great wife to his father, a fine mistress of Coronation Hill but she had never been a particularly good mother. For one thing she was absurdly wrapped up in him when sadly, she had spent little time or attention on her daughter, his younger sister, Meredith.

"Settle this for me, will you, son?" His father immediately drew him into an argument he and Ed were having about blood lines. The McKendricks had a passion for horses. Coronation Hill, named at the time of settlement in honour of the British queen, Victoria, was very serious about its breeding and training programme, not just for their own prized stockhorses, horses capable of dominating not only rodeos, gymkhanas and cross country events, but the racehorses on the bush circuit. Bush race meets were enormously popular, drawing people from all over the far-flung Outback.

Ewan clapped gleefully as Cal confirmed what he had been maintaining was correct. "Sorry, Uncle Ed." Cal slanted his gentle uncle a smile. "You were probably thinking of 'Highlander.' *He* was a son of 'Charlie's Pride.'"

"Of course." Edward nodded his head several times. Edward had never been known to best his elder brother. Though the family resemblance between the brothers was strong, Edward had always been outshone by Ewan in all departments, except Cal thought, in sensitivity and the wonderful ability to communicate with children and people far less fortunate than the grand McKendricks.

"Thanks for arriving just in time," his father crowed, giving his loud hearty laugh and stabbing a triumphant finger at his brother. "Fancy a cold beer, son? I know G&T's aren't your tipple."

"I'll go and get cleaned up first, Dad," Cal replied, quietly dismayed at how much pleasure his father took in putting his brother down.

"Did you sack young Fletcher?" Ewan grunted, shooting his son a startling, blue glance.

Cal shook his head, not prepared to alter his decision. "I've decided to give him another chance. He's young. He's learning. He takes the pain."

"Very well," was all his father said with a rough shake of his handsome head, when once he would have barked "You're not running Coronation yet, son."

Except these days he was, or close enough. It was, after all, his heritage. Irresistibly, Cal's gaze went to the series of tall arched stained-glass windows that dominated the library. The sinking sun was starting to stream through the glass, turning the interior of the huge room into a dazzling kaleidoscope of colour; ruby, emerald, sapphire, gold. Ceiling-high mahogany book-cases in colonnaded bays were built into the walls on three sides of the library housing a very valuable collection of books of all kinds: literature, world history, ancient and modern, mythology, science, valuable early maps, family documents, colonial history. It was a splendid collection that desperately needed cataloguing and maybe even re-housing. When his time came he would make it his business to hire someone well qualified to carry out this long-needed important work. Sadly neither his grandparents nor his father and mother had felt impelled to have the arduous task begun. Uncle Edward knew better than to interfere. Since he had tragically lost his wife to breast cancer ten years before, Ed had lived with the family.

Cal had no family of his own yet. No woman to share his life, ease the burden. Kym Harrison was the girl he was supposed to have married. He had been briefly engaged to her a couple of years back. He was still marvelling at how he had allowed it to happen. Of course, his mother had never let up on him to "tie the knot." But it hadn't been right for him and Kym deserved better.

Six months the engagement had lasted. Six months of fighting something too powerful to be overcome. Passion for another woman. One who had betrayed him. Every loving word that had fallen from her beautiful mouth had been a *lie*.

How could he have been so blindly mistaken? Even at near twenty-five he'd been no naive young fool. He was supposed to be, then as now, one of the most eligible bachelors in the country. He had to know it. The women's magazines kept him constantly in their lists. But there had been no serious attachment since. Just a few pain-free encounters, pain-free exits. Not that there was any such thing as safe sex. Someone always got hurt. It wasn't just a question of taking his time, either, of being *sure*. It was more a battle to exorcise those memories so vivid, they denied him the power to move on with his life. Yet he had tried.

He had known Kym since they were children. They connected on many levels. But compatibility, similar backgrounds, close family ties, weren't enough. Not for him anyway. Their relationship lacked what he had learned, to his cost, truly existed. *Passion*. Wild and ravishing; emotion that took you to the heavens then when it was ruthlessly withdrawn dropped you into your own pit in hell.

Hadn't he wanted her from the very first minute? The memory surfaced.

"Good morning, sir. Another glorious day!"

No shy dip of the head, but a calm, smiling, near-regal greeting, as if she were a princess in disguise. A princess, moreover, of uncommon beauty, even if she did happen to be folding towels.

He had stood there transfixed, desire pouring into him like burning lava. And it wasn't desire alone. He honestly felt he had no other choice but to fall madly in love with her. It was his fate. He hadn't been looking for any holiday fling; certainly not with a member of the island staff. Yet he had wanted this woman to have and to hold. *His woman*. God, in his secret heart she still remained *his woman*. What an agony love was! It forced itself on you, never to let go.

Gina!

How could he remain faithful if only in mind to a woman who had utterly deceived him? Kym had been his parents' choice almost from the cradle. Kym was the daughter of his mother's best friend, Beth Harrison. The Harrisons were their nearest neighbours on Lakefield. A marriage between them was a fantasy both mothers had harboured. His mother who had told him all his life she adored him—his mother was the classic type who doted upon the son—was still trying to come to terms with the split up. He had spent most of his childhood fighting off his mother's possessiveness, so it had been almost a relief to go away to boarding school even if it meant leaving his beloved Coronation Hill. How differently his mother had treated Meredith! Not unkindly, heavens no, she loved Meredith in her way, but rather as though daughters didn't matter all that much in the scheme of things. His mother's special love had been directed to *him*.

No little girl child should have to suffer that, he thought. When he married and children came along he would make sure any daughter of his would be treasured. Kym, an only child, enjoyed full parental love. It had been lavished on her. No son had come along in the Harrison family so Kym would inherit Lakefield. "You couldn't find a better match, my darling," his mother always told him. "No other woman could love you more than Kym does. Outside me, of course." This with a bright laugh. "Kym is perfect for you."

His mother didn't know about Gina unless his aunt Lorinda had told her. Lorinda had sworn she wouldn't. Lorinda, his mother's only sibling had helped him in a remarkable way back then. He was very grateful to her for her kindness and empathy. She always had been enormously supportive. It had to be true about Kym's really caring for him. They were still friends, despite everything. Or maybe Kym was just hanging in there until such time he realised she really was his best choice. Maybe compatibility could be made to work. Obsession after all, was a disaster. He gave a small shake of his head, warding his visions off. How could a man keep a woman's image burning bright when it was all of four years since her desertion? He had taken Gina's betrayal not just hard. It had near crushed the life out of him when up to then he had shown no fear of anything.

He had hated her at first. He had thought hate was a way out. But hate hadn't worked. Having loved her, he found it was less corrosive to hate himself. That's when he had allowed himself to become engaged to Kym, convincing himself Kym was the path to healing. That hadn't worked, either. It was just as impossible to remove Gina from his bloodstream as live without a heart.

He was passing his father's study when Meredith called to him, "Got a minute, Cal?"

"Sure." He walked into the room, his eyes ranging over her face. Usually his sister had a welcoming smile for him, but this afternoon she looked serious, even sad.

"Hey there, what's up?" His voice echoed his concern. Meredith was three years his junior. They were the best of friends. In fact, he would have to think really hard to remember a cross word between them. Their isolated upbringing had forged strong personal loyalties between them. He had always looked out for his little sister, though, like all the McKendricks Meredith had grown tall with the slim, lithe build of the athlete she was.

She was a marvellous horsewoman. She had won many cups and ribbons over the years, nearly as many as he had but no one had thought to display them as they did his. Once when they were kids, he had pinned her ribbons and rosettes all over her and taken pictures of her, both on and off her horse. He had hung on to those early photographs, too. The best one he'd had enlarged and framed. It sat on the desk in his bedroom along with a few other family portraits of them both. Great shots all of them.

He had to admit all his family were exceptionally good-looking. Genes were responsible for that. Meredith was beautiful but she made no effort to play up her looks. Rather she seemed to work at playing them down. She wore no make-up, just sunscreen and a touch of lipstick, jeans, neat little cotton shirts, her rich brown hair bleached gold at the temples by the sun, pulled back into a section of thick plait that ended in a loose ponytail. Even without her making the slightest effort, men turned to look at her.

There were lots of things he wished for his sister—a fuller more rewarding life, a man she could love and who loved her, marriage, children, but none of this was happening. For *either* of them. His father had frightened most of Meredith's serious suitors off. Their dad could be a very intimidating man. Although, it wasn't as if Meredith was the apple of his eye as any-one might expect with an only daughter. Meredith came well down the line when she should have been right up there. But that's the way it was. Nothing he nor Meredith could do about it. He was eternally grateful she had never blamed him. There had been no sibling rivalry, no wrenching jealousy. It had been bred into Meredith that sons not daughters were the ones who counted. As for suitors, most guys knew not to apply unless they could come up to scratch, and McKendricks' scratch was a very hard call.

"Take a look at this," Meredith was saying, breaking into his reverie. She laid a sheet of newspaper flat on the massive partner's desk, smoothing the crumpled surface. Such graceful hands, he thought, but regretfully getting knocked about with hard work. His sister did a lot more than pull her weight. She handled most things so quietly and effortlessly her capabilities tended to be overlooked or at the very least taken for granted. Meredith was not only beautiful but she had brains to spare. She would make some lucky guy a brilliant partner.

"What is it?" He rounded the desk, to stand beside her, topping her easily. "Oh, my God!" He felt the ground open up beneath his feet....

Watching him keenly, Meredith's face filled with anxiety. "Look, I'm sorry if I've done the wrong thing, Cal. But something inside told me you'd want to see this."

Physically and mentally reeling, he still managed to put a reassuring hand on her arm. "That's okay, I do."

"I thought so," Meredith breathed more easily. "You really loved her, didn't you?" She glanced at her brother's strong profile, registering his shock, and the way the muscles had bunched along his strong jawline.

"It's been a job trying to hate her," he answered, trying to control the grating harshness of his tone. He stared down at the beautiful unsmiling face of the girl in the newspaper photograph. "I always knew this day would come."

"I think I did, too," Meredith murmured quietly.

"How did you get a hold of it?" He glanced at the top of the page, seeing it was a Queensland newspaper. The State of Queensland adjoined the Northern Territory. They didn't take this newspaper.

"It came wrapped around some supplies Dad ordered," she said. "I almost screwed it up and threw it away. Something stopped me." Meredith paused, involuntary tears welling into her deep blue eyes. "She's still as beautiful as ever. More so now she's a woman. The first time I saw her back on the island I thought she looked like a very young Roman goddess. Full of grace, but there she was beavering away as a domestic. She had such a *look* about her."

"Enough to stop your breath." His mouth had turned so dry it was difficult to speak.

"I so liked her," Meredith lamented, even now wondering how she could have been so mistaken in Gina. "She seemed as beautiful inside as out."

"Error of judgement," he said with a humourless laugh. "I just couldn't believe it when Lorinda told me Gina had gone." Cal made a big effort to shove the old agony away. "She didn't even bother to give notice. She just took off."

Meredith recalled it well, her own shock and dismay, as Cal continued speaking. "The odd thing was Management didn't seem perturbed about it, when anyone would have thought they would be angry at the way she'd left them in the lurch. I could never figure it out."

"Aunt Lorinda would have had a private word with them," Meredith said quietly, "or her pal did. Ian Haig owned the island. Still does. Obviously to avoid further upsetting you, they dropped it."

"I guess so," Cal said, nodding. How did one learn to shut down on images that persisted? In his mind's eye, he saw Gina lying back on the white sand, the sea breeze all around them, him bending over her, ready to claim that lovely, moulded mouth. "We've been there, Mere." He sighed. "No one is going to take the ground from under my feet again. No point in going over it. Whatever the full story, Lorinda tried to help in any way she could."

"Not much use, was she?"

Cal's mahogany head, sun streaked like his sister's, jerked towards her in surprise. "What is that supposed to mean?"

"Well, she could have persuaded Gina to at least attempt to explain herself to you," Meredith said. "I would have, but Gina didn't confide in me. As for Aunt Lorinda, I haven't exactly forgiven her for interfering in my pitiful fling with Jake Ellory."

Cal grunted, "Ellory wasn't half good enough for you, Mere." He lay a sympathetic hand on her shoulder.

"Okay." She had to acknowledge that. "Point is I was able to see that for myself. I know Aunt Lorinda means well. She dotes on you, always has. She's very nice to me, too, but she's a master manipulator just like Mum. They're as thick as thieves. The facts were she was all in favour of Kym. Kym was the blue-eyed girl. Gina was the seductress. I guess we're never going to know exactly what happened. I could have sworn Gina was as madly in love with you as you were with her. The *feeling* that was generated between you two turned the air electric!"

"That wasn't electricity, my dear, that was hot air," Cal said flatly, his handsome features grown taut. "Gina didn't have the guts to tell me what she told Lorinda. What she had going was a great holiday fling. The reality was, she already had her serious boyfriend back home. Italian descent just like her. Marrying him was obviously very important in her family."

Meredith could accept that as true. Italian and Greek communities were very close. "Well, it was a sad, sad business. That's all I can say. But how does someone who readily puts her life on the line for a child act in a spineless manner? It doesn't make sense. Look at her face. It's not just a beautiful face, it's a *brave* face. I'm not surprised she did something like this. I can see her doing it, can't you? Why then didn't she try to explain herself? Why did she allow herself to get in so deep in the first place, given she was virtually promised to someone else? Perhaps she was frightened of her dad? I got the impression from something she let drop, he was super strict. I know all about strict dads."

Cal, re-reading the article, turned his remarkable gaze back on her.

A McKendrick in every other respect, the height, the splendid physique, the handsomely chiselled features, Cal had inherited his emerald-green eyes from their mother. Devil-green one of Meredith's girlfriends called them, always trying to capture Cal's attention with her bold, sexy glances.

"I'm going after her," he announced.

"You are?" Somehow that didn't shock her. She even wondered if she hadn't deliberately set it up. She could have thrown away the article. Instead she had kept it for him. Was it possible this time he and Gina could make it work? Gina's wedding plans with her Italian boyfriend hadn't come off it seemed.

"You bet!" Cal rasped, radiating determination. "How come she didn't marry that guy? It says here, Gina Romano." He stabbed the paper with a tanned forefinger. "That's her maiden name, not Gina Falconi, or Marente or whatever. Another guy she left with a broken heart. She's still unmarried. I want to know *why*." Cal threw up his head, unable to control the thoughts of revenge.

Meredith made no attempt to dissuade him. Cal had the bit between his teeth. When Cal decided to do something, it was done and pretty damned quick. She knew Gina had broken his heart. She knew he had been trying to forget her ever since. He deserved the chance to find out once and for all if Gina Romano simply wasn't worth all his pain. Cal was approaching thirty. He had to move on. Their parents were desperate for him to get married. They needed Cal to produce an heir, give them their first grandchild. Needless to say they would be hoping for a boy.

"What are you going to tell Mum and Dad?" she asked. "You run the station. You can't just vanish."

"I'm going to tell 'em I'm in need of a short break," he answered tersely. "Steve can hold the fort while I'm gone. He's well capable of it. He carries his old man's genes, even if Lancaster won't acknowledge him." Everyone in the Outback knew Gavin Lancaster, Channel Country cattle baron, was Steve Lockhart's biological father. Steve might as well have had *Lancaster* stamped on his forehead. "Even Dad concedes Steve has turned out just fine when initially he was against taking him on. Didn't want to get on the wrong side of Lancaster I suppose. Lancaster's one mean man."

Meredith's expression was wry. "They call Dad a son of a bitch behind his back," she reminded him.

"Maybe. But he's not *mean.* Mostly he's generous. Steve is shaping up to be the best overseer we've ever had. Had he been granted a bit of Lancaster money he could have bought a property of his own and worked it up."

"Well, that's not going to happen," Meredith spoke briskly, hoping the heat she felt in her veins didn't show in her cheeks. "Gavin Lancaster will go to his grave refusing to acknowledge Steve. One wonders why. His wife is dead. His other son doesn't measure up from all accounts. One can only feel sorry for him. Ah, well!" Meredith threw the issue off with a shrug. Usually she kept her thoughts about Steve Lockhart under wraps. She had learned the hard way to feign indifference to any man who attracted her, a man, moreover, who was a McKendrick employee and Gavin Lancaster's illegitimate son to boot. As far as her parents were concerned there was a *huge* gulf between family and staff. She found life easier if she kept up a pretence. No one was to know what went on inside her.

"I'll take this," Cal was saying, folding the sheet of newspaper so it fitted into the back pocket of his jeans.

"Be my guest. I suppose this just *could* be a mistake, Cal," she offered gently, feeling a sudden obligation to warn this brother she so loved and respected.

"That's just a chance I'm going to have to take." Cal started to move off, his stride swift and purposeful. At the door he turned to give her his heart-stopping smile. It was a smile Meredith shared, though she wasn't fully aware of it.

"It's been four years?"

"It only seems like yesterday."

Meredith blinked rapidly at the expression in his eyes. She knew the struggle he was having trying to keep his passionate emotions in check. The newspaper clipping had come as a revelation. "What are you going to do when you find her?" She realised she actually *wanted* Gina Romano back in their lives. Her memories of Gina were of a beautiful young woman strong but gentle with a great sense of humour and highly intelligent. The sort of young woman she would have treasured as a friend. She knew she couldn't speak for her mother and father. She had the sinking feeling they would be strongly against someone like Gina. Gina wasn't a PLU. It was the snob thing, PLU meaning People Like Us.

Cal took a moment to reply. "I'm going to demand she tell me to my face why she *lied*."

The words were delivered with chilling force.

CHAPTER TWO

GINA parked outside "Aunt" Rosa's modest bungalow made beautiful by the garden Rosa lavished such love and attention on. Taking the myriad scents of the garden deep into her lungs, Gina walked slowly up the stone-paved path to the front porch decorated with flower-filled hanging baskets. When Rosa had bought the bungalow three years back, Gina had helped greatly with the clean-up operation, cajoling a few of her sturdy male friends to join in, especially when it came to hauling in the rocks Rosa had used as natural features. In those days there was *no* garden, a few straggly plants, but Rosa had turned the allotment into a private garden paradise. The stone paths led through a wealth of flowering shrubs, camellias, azaleas, peonies, hydrangeas, through cascading archways of roses, all strongly fragrant, the floribunda wisteria, "Alba" and groves of lush ferns. There was always something happening in Rosa's garden, something to lift the heart.

Rosa was her godmother, her mother's bridesmaid at her first disastrous marriage which had produced Sandro and her. The great tragedy of her life was the disappearance of Sandro, her brother. Two years her senior he had run off at the age of sixteen after a violent argument with their father, the most difficult and demanding of men. Sandro had not only run off, he had vanished from the face of the earth. How did one do that? Gina had asked herself that question countless times. How did one lose one's identity? How did one go about obtaining a driving licence? What about credit cards, a Medicare card? Could Sandro be dead? Something inside her told her, no, though he had never contacted her or their mother to tell her he was safe, not a single phone call or a postcard. His disappearance had almost killed their mother and caused her, his loving sister, deep grief that continued right up to the present day.

Rosa knew all about her family's deeply troubled past. Rosa had been there. "One day, *cara*, Sandro will return to us. You'll see. It was just that he could no longer live with your father." What Rosa felt Gina's father to be was always delivered in impassioned Italian. Rosa was a woman of volatile temperament.

Yet their father had worshipped her, his daughter. She could do no wrong. She was his shining star. She might have been marked down for future canonisation. *"My beautiful Gianina!"* Until the night she confessed she was pregnant. Then her virgin image had been well and truly shattered.

Rosa had always kept in touch with her. Indeed, Rosa had offered to take her in, after her father had literally thrown her, the fallen idol, out. It had truly been the never-darken-my-door-again situation she had hitherto thought only existed in novels. But the last thing she had wanted was to bring down trouble on Rosa's head even though her godmother had sworn she could handle the likes of Ugo Romano.

"He's a great big bully, you know!"

When Primo, Rosa's husband, died at the early age of fifty-four Rosa sold the old sugar farm and travelled to Brisbane to be near her goddaughter. Rosa, a warm, generous woman had not been blessed with children, a great sorrow to her. *"Poor Primo, he couldn't manage it."* Otherwise Primo had been a good, good man. Everyone in the community had agreed on that.

"Someone has to look after you!" Rosa announced when she arrived on Gina's doorstep, followed by a torrent of curses aimed at Gina's father. At least one of them must have worked because Gina's father barely eighteen months later had bounced off a country road, the old farm utility turning over a few times before landing in a ditch killing him in the process.

"God has spoken," Rosa, never short of an explanation, pronounced at the funeral. *"Now everyone is safe. My poor Lucia, maybe, might find herself another husband. One to cherish her. I see Vince Gambaro over there."*

Gina's mother, Lucia, was pardoned by both her daughter and Rosa. Though desperately unhappy in her arranged marriage, she had been too cowed by her husband to leave him though the friends who cared for her had begged her to do so.

"Sometimes poison isn't all that bad!" muttered Rosa, with black humour.

Before Gina was even at the door, painted cobalt-blue and flanked by matching glazed pots bearing a wealth of pink camellias, Rosa, unconventionally, but eye-catchingly dressed in her own creations, was out on the porch, smiling a welcome.

"He just loves this cartoon," she said. "Lots of giggles, clapping, singing, dancing, peals of laughter. Such a beautiful sound, a child's laughter! I think the video is nearly through."

"Has he been a good boy?" Gina bent to kiss her godmother's satin-smooth cheek. Rosa was a striking-looking woman with a passionate, lived-in kind of face. She was also very queenly in a gypsy fashion. And she had admirers. Rosa had always had admirers, though she had never once succumbed to temptation in all the years of her marriage. One admirer was very much in the picture, a well-to-do widower, a retired bank manager. Gina had met him on several occasions, thinking him a nice man but lacking Rosa's broad cultural interests.

"Always a good boy! Impossible not to love him." Rosa was stroking Gina's arm, showing the depth of her affection. Her goddaughter had filled a vacuum in Rosa's life, but nothing could erase the sorrow of not having children and grandchildren of her own. Gina and Roberto came somewhere in between.

"Mummy!" Now Robbie was at the door, holding up his arms.

Gina picked him up and hugged him to her while he covered her cheeks in kisses. "Hello, my darling," she said, her heart melting with love. "So what happened at preschool today?"

"I learnt lots of things," he told her proudly, then frowned. "I think I've forgotten now."

"No matter. It will all come back."

"Are you coming in?" Rosa asked, standing back from the door.

"For ten minutes," Gina smiled. "I've got something for you."

"For me, too?" Robbie asked hopefully.

"Something for you *both*," Gina said setting her son down. Goodness he was getting heavy and he was tall for his age.

"I hope mine comes in a bottle," Rosa flashed another dark-eyed grin. Rosa was a wonderful cook and something of a wine expert, partial to a really good red, preferably a Shiraz.

"It got highly rated," Gina told her

"Bellisimo!" Rosa cried, throwing up her arms and going into a spirited little dance that made the gold hoops in her ears sway and Robbie laugh. Rosa was far more of a grandmother to Robbie than ever his real grandmother was, now living far away on a New Guinea coffee plantation.

They walked through to the kitchen, Robbie running ahead. Modest from the outside, inside the bungalow was a reflection of Rosa's exuberant, artistic nature. The walls of the house were covered in her paintings. The warmly welcoming yellow-and-white kitchen was dominated by a large painting of a wicker basket filled to overflowing with yellow lemons and their lustrous leaves, the leaves spilling on to a white tablecloth. Gina loved it. Rosa had given her several of her paintings to decorate the apartment.

They were home in less than ten minutes. She settled Robbie in front of the television in the living room so he could watch the end of the video while she went through to her bedroom to change out of her smart business clothes. Inside the walk-in wardrobe she reached for a comfortable caftan that was still rather glamorous, fuchsia silk with a gold trim. She'd been out to a business lunch, which she thought should carry her through dinnertime. Maybe a light salad? Robbie wanted his all-time favourite which she allowed him once a week—sausages and mash. She always bought the best quality pork sausages, wrapped them in bacon, which he liked and let him have tomato sauce, which surprise, surprise, had turned out to be one of the dwindling number of things good for everyone. Once a very fussy eater, Robbie now enjoyed his food, eating the healthiest food for most of the time. The great news was she now had him eating banana porridge before he went off to school. He refused point-blank to eat cereal or eggs. *Yuck!*

She was passing through the hallway when a knock on the apartment door startled her. Visitors had to buzz through to her video-intercom and identify themselves before being allowed through the security door. It had to be Dee from the Body Corporate Management. If parcels arrived and couldn't be delivered because she was at work, Dee usually took care of them. Dee was a good sort, ever helpful, kind and gentle with Robbie. And why not? Her beautiful little son was a gorgeous child with the sunniest of natures. Everyone loved him.

She didn't open the door immediately. She checked through the peephole but could only see someone holding up a large bouquet of yellow roses. They looked like her favourite, *Pal Joey*. Nat Goldman, a very nice guy she worked with, had taken to sending her roses, but they were usually red. Shaking back the long tumble of her hair, she threw back the door, a smile on her face.

And there was Calvin McKendrick; the power elite!

There had been no icy tingle this time to warn her. Her powers had deserted her. Or his powers were stronger. The blood roared in her ears and she wrapped her arms tightly around herself as if the action could prevent her from falling. No trace of her smile remained.

Four years were as *nothing*. His presence was as vividly familiar to her as if their separation had only been fleeting moments. Yet she stood rooted to the spot, unable to move, unable to speak, struck dumb with wonderment. Then very gradually her entire body began to react. She felt an unbearable urge to throw herself into his arms, feel them close powerfully around her. She wanted to inhale his marvellous male scent. She wanted to kiss his beautiful mouth. She wanted to *taste* him. Hadn't she suffered grievously these past years? Instead she took a long, deep breath, widening her eyes in surprise.

"Cal!"

"Ah, you've remembered!" he said suavely. "Do please go on." There was a dangerous edge to the civility of his tone. It matched the glitter in his remarkable eyes, as green as emeralds, and as cold.

"Go on?" She groped for the door behind her so she could close it. He couldn't be allowed to see Robbie. She had to keep him from it. She was too frighteningly vulnerable, now as then. He could take her beloved son off her, or curtail her time with him. That prospect she couldn't bear. The McKendricks were powerful people with an army of lawyers at their disposal and limitless funds. That alone inspired fear.

"Well, surely you're going to add you're surprised to see me?" The voice she had so loved, was filled with mockery.

"I am, *very!*" Even to her own ears her voice sounded strangled. She was trembling all over, her heart kicking against her ribs. "How did you find me?"

He tut-tutted. "And you, the heroine?"

Of course. The newspaper story that had even made it onto the television. People still pointed at her in the street. Some even came up to her, congratulating her on her bravery.

What can I do? She couldn't get her head around the dilemma that now faced her. It was imperative she pull herself together.

"Have you someone with you?" he asked, seeing the agitation that was written all over her. His eyes went beyond her to the entrance hall; a small console, a striking oil painting above it, two Victorian lustres, emerald-green glass, decorated with tiny white flowers and gold leaves; all very pretty.

Gina scrambled to nod her head, though she felt dazzled and dazed.

"Are you asking me to come back another time?" Perversely he found his eyes consuming her. She was a wonderful-looking woman; more beautiful than ever, if that were possible. Her classical features were more clearly defined, her eyes, deep, dark bottomless pools. Her masses of hair, neither straight nor curly, fell in thick sinuous coils halfway down her back. Desire over which he had no control streamed through his blood, like a river in full spate. He was a greater fool than even he had thought.

"Please don't come back, Cal," Gina begged, spinning very quickly as she heard Robbie, his programme over, moving to join her. "There's absolutely nothing we could have to say to one another after all this time." Galvanised, she tried to shut the door but Cal deliberately blocked her efforts with one foot against it.

No, Robbie! The voice inside her shrieked.

But Robbie came on, dead-set on finding out who his mother was talking to. Robbie had great social skills. He loved visitors. Just as she feared, he rounded the partition that divided the entrance hall from the living area, running to Gina and grasping her around the hips. "Hello!" he said brightly, addressing Cal. "Are you a friend of Mummy's?" He gave an engaging little chuckle, looking at Cal with the greatest interest.

But Cal for once in his life was literally struck dumb. He stood pulverized by shock. Whatever scenarios he had considered on his long trip here, it was never this! He found himself rocking back on his heels as the truth came roaring for him like an express train.

God! There was nothing irreverent about his silent oath. Recognition shot simultaneously to his heart and his brain. This was his child. This was his son! There could be no mistake. The child resembled him too closely.

He dragged his eyes away from the beautiful little boy, to pin Gina's treacherous, dark gaze. She looked frightened, utterly wretched, as well she might! "I'd like to come in, if I may." He fought to keep the tight rein on his voice, for the child's sake. "It seems, Gina, we have things to discuss." He put out his hand to his son: dark copper curls like petals, framing an angelic little face. In adolescence those dark copper curls would turn a rich mahogany like his. He had the McKendrick features, but even more tellingly the black-lashed eyes so brilliant a green, they were often described as emerald. There was the McKendrick cleft in his chin, not deep like his father's, more shallow like his. Uncle Ed had a cleft chin. Meredith had a distinctive dimple.

"Hello there, Robbie." Cal showed the child all the gentleness and warmth he denied the mother. "I'm Cal. Calvin McKendrick.

I am an old friend of your mother's. I'm so very pleased to meet you at long last, though I think I would have known you anywhere." Anywhere on this earth, he thought, trying to come to grips with Gina's treachery.

"And I'm pleased to meet *you*," Robbie responded, sweetly, unlocking his grasp on his mother and extended his hand as he'd been taught.

Cal thrust the beautiful yellow roses into Gina's rigid arms before taking the child's hand. "So, Robert?"

"*Robbie.* I've been watching my favourite cartoon."

"Really?" Cal spoke normally, though naked shock was showing in his eyes.

"You can see my video if you like," Robbie offered graciously.

"That's very nice of you, Robbie," Cal said.

"Have you got time now?" the little boy asked hopefully, obviously having taken an immediate liking to Cal.

"Darling," Gina interrupted, "Cal only called in for a minute." She drew Robbie back against her, giving Cal a pleading look.

It had no effect on Cal whatsoever. "No, that's okay!" He shrugged a rangy shoulder. "I wasn't going anywhere special. Do you mind, Robbie, if I come in?" Cal gave his son an utterly winning smile.

"Oh, *please*, Mummy, can he?" Robbie stared up into his mother's face, a highly intelligent child, trying to puzzle out the atmosphere. "I haven't had my tea yet," he told Cal. "It's bangers and mash. Would you like some?"

"If there's any to spare." Cal twisted Gina a hard, challenging smile. He was absolutely certain he wouldn't be able to eat anything, but he definitely wasn't going away.

"Oh, goody!" Robbie put out his hand to take Cal's. "Oh, your hands are rough inside!" he burst out in surprise, as baby soft three-year-old fingers met up with hard calluses.

"That's because I'm a cattleman," Cal explained.

"What's that, a cattleman?" Robbie asked with great interest, beginning to pull Cal through the door. "Do you own cattle, cows and things?"

Cal nodded. "One day I'll show you."

"Promise?" Robbie's big beautiful eyes lit up.

"Let's shake on it."

"You're a very nice man," Robbie pronounced, taking the handshake as a promise.

"Thank you," Cal replied. "It must be getting along to your bedtime soon?" he asked, desperate to have it out with this woman who had so betrayed him.

"Seven o'clock." Robbie lifted his head to scan the face of this tall man he seemed to know somehow, but couldn't understand why. "That's when I go to preschool. I can stay up a little later at the week-end. Will you be here when I go to sleep?"

"Bound to be," Cal said.

Somehow they kept up a reasonable pretence until Robbie went to bed. His mother kissed him as she always did when she tucked him in. "Good night, my darling."

"'Night, Mummy."

"Sleep tight."

"Don't let the bed bugs bite." Robbie giggled as he finished off the nightly ritual, then he put out a hand to Cal.

"You're going to come back and see us, aren't you, Cal?" he asked hopefully.

"Count on it."

Gina watched Cal lean down and touch her little boy's cheek with the most exquisite tenderness.

"That's good. I really like you," Robbie said, the glow from the bedside lamp turning his eyes to jewels.

"As it happens I really like you." Cal smiled, watching his son sigh contentedly, then close his eyes, dark lashes heavy on apricot cheeks.

They returned in a fraught silence to the living room. Gina was amazed tears weren't streaming down her cheeks. She had never seen Robbie respond to anyone like he had to Cal.

Blood will out!

Carefully, she shut the door that led down the corridor to the bedrooms, grateful Robbie slept very soundly, especially when he was overexcited as he was tonight.

"You hate me," Gina said. His face was a taut mask.

"Who in hell would blame me?" Cal replied in a tone so contemptuous it cut deep. "Why did you do it?" He went to her and seized her arms with controlled fury. "So you ran back to your boyfriend! Why didn't you make a fool of him like you made a fool of me? When you realised it was my child you were carrying, why didn't you try to pass it off as his? Didn't think you'd be able to pull if off, eh? Worried he might kill you when he eventually found out? Where did the green eyes come from, the copper curls? Robert is the image of me when I was his age. I have stacks of photographs to prove it, as though we *need* proof." He released her so abruptly, Gina stumbled and had to clutch at the back of an armchair to stay upright.

"I'm sorry if you feel hurt, Cal," she said, tonelessly. "At least it proves you're human."

"Human? What the hell are you talking about? And you're *sorry?* God!" He began to pace the carpet like a caged tiger. "Is that all you can say, sorry? I had a right to *know.* Robert is three years old. Just think what I've missed! Or haven't you any heart at all? For three years I've had a son I didn't even know existed. I wasn't there when he was born, when he took his first steps, when he started to say his first words. I've missed his birthdays.

I've missed loving him. I've missed the joy of having him love me. What's wrong with you? How could you do that to me?" He fell down on the sofa, throwing back his head and covering his eyes with his hands. "What the hell were you thinking about? Dear God, Gina, are you devoid of all conscience?"

She stared back at him, trying hard not to burst into tears. "Don't, please *don't!* I had to cope any way I could."

He flung up his handsome head, tension making his features more hawklike than ever. "And that meant absenting me from your life?" He stared about him at the large room, decorated with style and care, the furnishings, the art works, the fresh flowers. "You live here?"

"Of course I live here." She thrust the heavy fall of her hair over her shoulder.

"Alone with Robert?" He shot her a challenging glace.

"Yes." She dared not add "As if it's any of your business." He was furious, shocked, a pallor beneath his dark tan. She was frightened of him; of what he might do. She just knew something was going to come of that newspaper article.

"You work?" The question was terse. "Sit down, why don't you?"

Demolished she took a seat opposite him. Her heart was beating so fast she thought she might be sick. Low voiced, she named her firm of stockbrokers.

"It must be a darn good job!" He let his eyes move insolently around the attractively furnished room.

"It is," she answered shortly, regaining her breath. "All you see here is mine."

"Bravo!" he crowed.

"What do you want, Cal?" She cut across him, the room thick with tension.

"Who looks after Robert until you get home?" His eyes lanced.

She hated this interrogation, even as she knew she had to endure it. "My godmother, Rosa. She's a wonderful woman. Roberto loves her."

"What's the wonderful Rosa doing down here in Brisbane, or is *everything* you told me a pack of lies?"

"No!" she protested, shaking her head. "When Rosa's husband died she sold the farm to be near me. She takes her responsibilities as godmother very seriously."

"Her prayers couldn't prevent you becoming an inveterate liar," he countered bitterly.

"I never lied to you."

He laughed harshly. "God, you're lying *now.* You were the one who told me you loved me. You told me you never dreamed there could be such happiness. You told me you wanted to be with me always. If they weren't lies, may I ask what in hell *were* they?"

Fearful only a moment before, Gina's magnificent dark eyes flashed. "Why weren't *you* truthful with me?" she demanded, the pain of the past as raw as yesterday. "You had a girl back home you were expected to marry. I even know her name, Kym Harrison. Don't look so shocked. Men are notoriously unfaithful. I saw a photograph of you together in a magazine. You were at the Melbourne Cup. Calvin McKendrick and his lovely fiancée, Kym Harrison. I still have the clipping somewhere to remind me of your treachery. Why didn't you tell me about your Kym?"

He couldn't answer for a minute so taken aback was he by her use of the word *treachery.* "Why are you drawing Kym into this?" he retaliated, heavily frowning. "As soon as I met you there *was* no other woman. No Kym. You were everything I wanted. *My* woman. Getting engaged to Kym came after. It shames me to say it, it certainly wasn't my finest moment, but I became engaged to Kym to forget *you!*"

She stared at him, this man who had haunted her, the father of her child. "It didn't work?" Her tone was deeply hostile. She was out to wound as he was wounding her.

"No more than your relationship with your Italian boyfriend," he countered, sending her a glittering glance that would have crushed her, only she was too startled by his mention of a boyfriend.

"I beg your pardon?" she said, disdainfully, lifting her chin.

He laughed at the hauteur. "Oh, come off it! How easily you assume the regal demeanour. Sure there's not a Contessa or two in the background?"

"I wish!" There was a curl of her moulded lips. Those lips he had kissed so often. "I had *no* Italian boyfriend if that's your idea of an excuse. My father frowned on boyfriends. I was a virgin when I met you. You *know* that."

Colour mounted to his prominent cheekbones. "Yes," he admitted, "but we did use protection."

"One time we didn't."

He buried his head in his hands. "Then my responsibility was far greater than yours. You were just a girl. I was mad about you. Absolutely crazy with love and longing. The last thing I wanted to do was hurt you."

"Am I supposed to believe that?" Her tongue lashed him. "You *did* hurt me. More than you will ever know. I've suffered, but I have my beautiful Roberto."

"And Robert is a McKendrick family name. I recall telling you that."

"Maybe you did—" she shrugged "—but I named him after my brother, Alessandro. Roberto is his middle name." She didn't tell him both factors had influenced her.

Cal studied her with a frown, suddenly remembering how she had told him an older brother had defected from home. "You're talking about the Sandro who went missing when he was sixteen?"

"Aah! You actually remember something!" Her voice throbbed with scorn.

"I remember *everything!*" he corrected her harshly. "He's never contacted you?"

She shook her head, sadness replacing the scorn. There was a long, long list of Missing Persons. "He could be dead for all we know."

Even through his shock and anger, her obvious sorrow reached him.

Gina swallowed on a dry throat. Before her she saw a man who had matured a good deal since she had last seen him. He looked every inch a man of power and authority. The sweetness, however, that had been so much part of his expression had disappeared.

The fear returned. "Please, Cal. Can you reassure me you wouldn't be so cruel as to try to take Robbie from me. I adore him. He's my son."

"He's *my* son, too, Gina," he said curtly, rising to his feet and looming over her. "Tonight I claim him. Fortune has at long last decided to turn my way. I have every intention of taking him back to Coronation Hill. He's a McKendrick. Coronation is his home. It's his heritage. He's my heir."

Anger and fear boiled together in her great dark eyes. "He's my heir, too, I remind you! Romano blood runs in my son's veins. Just when do you think you could take him? Go on, tell me that. And what about me? Do you really think I'm going to stand back and let you take Roberto from me? You'd have to kill me first."

His expression, unlike hers, was astoundingly cool. He took hold of her wrist, letting her feel just a touch of his vastly superior strength. "No need to kill you, Gina," he drawled. "*Marrying* you suits me better."

For a moment she thought she would faint. "Because I have

your child?" she cried passionately. "I wasn't good enough for you before." She pulled away violently, rubbing her wrist. "Marriage between us would never work."

He went down on his haunches before her. "Listen and listen carefully." He spoke softly but his demeanour conveyed forceful determination. "I want my son to have a proper upbringing. No broken home. I want him to have a mother and father. That's the two of us. Are you going to tell me there's someone else on the horizon? Someone prepared to take on another man's child? Not that he would have to. I'm intent on getting custody of Robert. I don't think the court would look too *favourably* on you and your deceit. Your brother, Sandro, isn't the only one in your family who likes to disappear. Tell me this? How can a woman who put her own life on the line to save a child, lack the guts to come forward? To stand up and be counted. Or were you overcome with guilt?"

She kept her head lowered, not daring to look into his mesmeric eyes. She was overwhelmingly conscious their faces were mere inches away. "Even when you were making love to me, making our baby, you were lying," she said wretchedly.

He made a sound of the greatest impatience. He caught her chin sharply, holding a hard thumb to it to keep it up. "You could get any acting job. You're great!" he scoffed. "It's the Italian thing. You know how to exploit emotion. I told you I loved you. I never meant anything more in my life. That part of it is over. I can never trust you again. These past four years I've learned to *hate!*"

"And I have hated, as well. A nice basis for a marriage!" Gina looked him right in the eye, her tone inflammatory. Damn him, damn him! Being so close to him was tearing her in all directions. "And what about your so lofty family?" she demanded. "They wouldn't have accepted me then, why now? Although I don't include your sister, Meredith, in this!"

He stood up, rigid with disgust. "Lord, what a fake you are, Gina. Don't try to drag my family into this. Why don't you just admit it? I was your last big fling before you settled down and became a good little Italian wife. You were going home to marry your boyfriend, the one *Papa and Mamma* had picked out for you." Unforgivably he parodied an Italian accent.

"You were the one going home to marry your Kym." Her great eyes flashed. "So you see, liars on both sides." Suddenly she saw clearly her version of events would clash with his own. She had had her knowledge from his aunt, but at this point she didn't want to draw his aunt into the whole tragic mess because it would only serve to further anger and alienate him.

"Well, we got our just reward," he said with deep irony. "My engagement didn't work. Your marriage prospects were doomed to failure. It's the old story, isn't it? Damaged goods. Hate that expression myself. I have to say motherhood has done wonders for you." He made it sound like she'd once been an ugly duckling. "The dewy girl has turned into a woman. You didn't answer me about your current love life? Not that it matters a damn whatever you're going to say."

She stared across at him, feeling a tightness in her chest. She had loved him as much as she was capable of loving anyone outside her son. *Their son.* "You're serious, then? You're going to force a marriage on me?"

"You bet!"

The hard light in his eyes swallowed all her breath.

"I seem to recall your telling me your parents' marriage was arranged?"

"And it was desperately unhappy as any marriage between us would be." Remembrance of her unhappy family life shadowed her face.

"You omitted to tell me that. I suppose another lie?"

"So, I'm an accomplished actress and an inveterate liar?" She gave him a scathing glance.

"Maybe the two sometimes go together! And how are the Romanos?" He used his suavest tone.

She was racked by a little convulsive shiver. "My father is dead. My mother has remarried. She and her husband live in New Guinea now. I rarely see her."

He lifted supercilious black brows. "She didn't waste much time?"

"She's trying to make up for the lost years," Gina said crisply. "My father had a very difficult temperament."

"I'm sorry to hear it. I suppose that's why Sandro took off?"

"My father was very hard on him. Not at all kind."

"Yet you gave me the strong impression he adored you?"

Adored her? When she exactly matched his vision of her. She sometimes thought her father couldn't have coped with a pregnant daughter, in or out of wedlock.

"What no answer?" He stared across at her, so wanting to pull her into his arms he had to grip the sides of his chair.

"I'm not going to allow you to question me further," she said angrily. "You McKendricks are cruel people."

That stung him. "Don't you think you should wait to meet them before you decide that?'

"I've met *you*." Her great dark eyes dominated her face. "Let me say again. A marriage between us couldn't work."

He steepled his lean hands, as though considering. "Given you're the mother of my son," he said finally, "I suggest you try to make it work. Or sit it out."

"Sit it out?" she gasped. "I would never, never choose to sit my life out. I want what every woman wants—a man to love her, children, a happy home. We have nothing in common."

"Apart from our son. Never forget that. And unless I'm very

much mistaken we're still physically attracted to one another. We could still have the sex. That might keep us pinned together. The sex hasn't gone away, has it?"

She could never deny it. But she *did*. "Oh, stop that!" she said sharply. "Sex is out of the question."

"But I've never forgotten it. You were terrific, Gina. I wanted you to the point of madness. Pathetic how you made me feel! You made me so weak with longing I couldn't see straight. I used to go around all the time my body aching with pain and desire. I was *nuts* about you." He could barely contain his hostility.

"But that was it, wasn't it?" she retorted. "You just loved having sex with me."

"Why not? Sex with you was Heaven. And so disastrous!"

"Some relationship!" she muttered bitterly. "Well, I paid for it."

"Not just *you!*" His expression hardened into granite. "If you can spare a thought for me, who was never told he was a father. How long will it take you to get yourself organised?" he asked crisply. "I assume you'll have to give notice to your firm. You'd better make it as short as you can. There'll be no difficulty taking Robert out of play school or whatever it is."

She put a hand to her pounding temples. "I can't do this," she near wailed. "You're quite mad."

"My dear Gina, I've never been saner." He leaned back in the armchair, the picture of nonchalance. "If you fight me I promise you, you'll lose. Your best course—indeed, your only course—is to try to make a go of this. *I'm* prepared to."

His arrogance made her livid. "*You're* prepared to!" She totally forgot herself and shouted.

"Keep it down," he warned, turning his head towards the bedroom area.

"Don't tell me what I should do in my own home," she hissed, saturated in hot feeling. "I can see you've grown ruthless."

"If I have it's because of you," he retorted on the instant. "If it makes you more comfortable I give you my solemn promise I won't touch you until you're ready."

"And what makes you think I'll *ever* be ready?" She stared at him coldly.

"Let's have a little test run, shall we?"

He confounded her by rising from his chair.

An unbelievable thrill shot through her. "No test runs!"

He hauled her to her feet, holding her so she had no chance of getting away. "Not so easy to run now, is it, *Gianina?*"

Passion came boiling to the surface. Will subservient to the flesh. Past merged into present. "Don't accuse me of running one more time," she gritted. She hadn't run. She'd been persuaded it was the only thing she could do. The honourable thing.

"Or you'll do what?" His eyes rested compulsively on her full mouth. "Don't try playing the innocent victim with me, Gina. It won't wash. You're a born seductress. You don't have to do anything but look at a man. *Kiss* me."

"Too many kisses," she said, yet her whole being was thrown into a sensual upheaval. No one touched her like he did. She tried to call on her pride and her sense of self-esteem. It would have been easier to call up thunder and lightning. "Damn you to hell!" she cried weakly as his grip tightened.

"I've been there." He spoke with great bitterness, sweeping her fully into his arms. There he held her as though that was where she belonged and nowhere else. She wondered how, after so much pain, her body could respond so brilliantly to his touch; but shamefully it did. It was no mock-up test kiss. It was incredibly turbulent, profoundly vengeful. Deeply suppressed emotions erupted as if at the touch of a detonator.

When they finally broke apart, both were breathing heavily. Cal waited only a speechless moment before he pulled her against him again. "So it's not all over then?" His emerald eyes glittered as though he had won an important battle.

How could she find the words to deny it anyway? He had ruined her utterly for other men. "You said it yourself. All we've got is sex."

"And it's *good*," he ground out harshly, before covering her mouth again.

Hungrily his hand sought her breast, shaped it, his fingers taking hold of the erect nipple, tightening *exquisitely.* She couldn't help her quick gasps that he muffled with his lips. There was a hot gush of feelings inside of her as powerful chemicals were released into her bloodstream.

Surely it was a type of cruelty this power he had over her? she thought fiercely. Would she never be safe from him, safe from herself?

It wasn't just Cal's strong arms that were holding her hostage. Gina could deny it all she liked, but it was her own heart.

Hours after he had gone back to his hotel, Gina lay in bed sobbing as she hadn't sobbed for years. All the suffering came back to haunt her. Her parents' unhappy marriage; her mother's inability to stand up for herself or for her children, in particular Sandro; her father's periodic rages and she the only one they were rarely directed at; Sandro's disappearance after that last dreadful fight. Later the miracle of the island that had touched her with such radiance, then left her an outcast. The terrifying discovery she was pregnant; her own banishment from the family home, the all pervading sense of loss. Just seeing Cal again brought it all rushing back like the incoming tide to the shore.

She could never have survived on her own without the small stash of money her mother had secreted from her father and stuffed inside a pocket of her suitcase, all the while crying broken-heartedly, without the courage to intervene. More financial help had come from Rosa and Primo; and all through, Rosa's tremendous support. Gina had known the background of her baby son's father, scion of a rich and powerful family, but she had never considered contacting him. She didn't need to be paid off. She had her pride to sustain her. The love she had felt for Cal McKendrick, the ruling passion that had altered the course of her life, was soured by betrayal.

In the last couple of years she had found her feet, but the memory of him had shadowed her life, making it near impossible for her to embark on another relationship. Now he had marched right back into her life, filled with a violent outrage she had kept the existence of his son from him. She tried to block out the harshness and devastation that had been in his voice. Did she really deserve such condemnation? Perhaps she did. She understood his pain even as she feared his power and influence. The time had come for him to assert his rights; to claim his son and as a consequence his son's mother.

"This time you're not getting away, Gina. You're going to do exactly what I tell you."

She rose from the bed to change her tear-drenched pillows, turning her head to look at her bedside clock. 2:10 a.m. She reminded herself she had to get up early in the morning. She had to shower and dress, wake Robbie, get his breakfast, then ready him for preschool, drop him off, then continue on into work where she had to do what he had instructed her to do. Hand in her notice.

CHAPTER THREE

YARDING up had gone on all day. Steve was closing the gates on the portable steel yard when she rode up on him. He knew even before he turned his head it was Meredith. That's how sensitised he was to her presence. She had helped out all day on a tough job. Too tough for a woman, he thought, but there was no dissuading her. She was a McKendrick. Most of the young guys on the station were in love with her. Fat lot of good it would do them, the only daughter of the "Duke and Duchess" Ewan and Jocelyn McKendrick.

"I think I can say it's been quite a day!" she sighed lustily from behind him.

"You did more than your fair share," he said as he turned, using a matter-of-fact voice. It was the usual way they talked to one another. Keep it businesslike. "Any news of Cal?"

She dismounted, and he took the reins from her, knotting them around a rung of the fence. "Plenty." She was dressed like he was, in jeans and a cotton shirt. He had a bold red bandana around his throat. Hers was blue to match her shirt, but the colour paled into insignificance against the sapphire of her eyes. Both of them wore cream felt Akubras low over their eyes. Even the late-afternoon sun had a real bite to it.

"Big secret, is it?"

She didn't smile and she had the most beautiful smile in the world. Lovely white teeth, finely cut mouth. An aristocrat yet with no vanity or ostentation. "I guess you're going to know about it soon enough," she said, "but I'd like you to keep it to yourself."

"Sure."

She nodded, knowing he was as close lipped as she was and very loyal. "Let's walk down to the creek, shall we?"

He dared not speak. What could he say? I'd walk to the ends of the earth with you? He'd been on Coronation Hill the best part of two years with hardly a day when she hadn't been stuck in his head. Truth be known he was well and truly smitten with Ms Meredith McKendrick. Enormous effrontery but he'd learned from early childhood how to cover up his feelings. The men, never slow to catch on, hadn't a clue, though Tom, the retiring overseer, had muttered to him just before he left: "Reckon you could handle McKendrick, son. Why don't you have a go?"

He would, too, only he had precious little to offer a woman like Meredith McKendrick. He couldn't even offer her a clean name. All because of Lancaster! It had been tough growing up, as he had, in a family with various shades of blond hair when his was as black as a crow's wing. His eyes instead of being the Lockhart's azure-blue were more gold than brown. Eyes were a dead give-away. They showed one's ancestry. Meredith, for instance, had the McKendrick eyes. They were so blue in some lights they looked purple. Cal had his mother's eyes—dark green with a jewel-like quality. Steve was barely ten when he discovered his "foreign" colouring didn't come from his mother's side of the family as she had always claimed. His colouring came directly from Gavin Lancaster.

He remembered hiding out on the verandah, listening to his mother crying in the bedroom until her tears must have blinded her. He remembered Jim Lockhart berating her, full of an impotent rage now the secret was out. No one could touch Gavin Lancaster. He was too powerful. But Gavin Lancaster could make life very hard for a stockman like Jim Lockhart and his family. He had two half brothers and a half sister. All of them, including his mother, had long since packed up and moved to New Zealand, putting the Tasman between them. The Outback was Lancaster's territory. A man needed to be frightened of Gavin Lancaster and his vengeance.

All except him. He sure as hell wasn't frightened. He had remained. No one was going to separate him from the land he loved. Certainly not the man who had sired him.

He followed Meredith's lead down to the bubbling stream, a small tributary of a much larger billabong, their boots bruising hundreds of tiny wildflowers he thought were native violets.

"Let's sit here," she said, sinking wearily onto the pale golden sand and throwing off her wide-brimmed hat. She had beautiful hair…long and thick and gleaming, burnished at the temples with streaks the colour of champagne. He would love to see it out, streaming over her shoulders. A dream?

Slowly, he lowered his long length beside her—he was six-three—relishing the moment but keeping a respectful distance. "Problems?" he asked, slanting her a glance. No one would have known he was suffocating inside, just to be near her. The two of them alone together. It rarely happened. He calmed himself, feeling the slick of sweat on his brow.

Meredith stared across the creek that could swell to a river in the Wet. The late-afternoon sun was flooding the area with light, throwing rose-gold bands across the rippling surface of the water. "I'm telling you this, Steven, because I trust you. Cal does, too."

She was the only one to ever call him Steven. He loved his own name on her lips. "You know anything you tell me remains private."

She nodded. "It will all come out eventually."

"It can't be that bad if it has to do with Cal?"

"I'm hoping with all my heart it will be good," she burst out emotionally. "This all has to do with a woman."

"Most things do." He sounded solemn.

"The only woman for Cal," Meredith said. "It started four years ago. Some of the family took a long holiday on a Barrier Reef island, a small privately run luxury resort. A friend of my aunt's owns it. Our group, extended family and friends took over the island. It only caters to around thirty. On the island was a very beautiful young woman called Gina. She was working in the university vacation as a domestic, waitress, whatever was required. Cal fell madly in love with her and I could have sworn she fell madly in love with him. It was really something to see them together."

"Sounds like it ended badly?" he said, feeling truly sorry. How could anything end badly with a guy like Cal McKendrick who had everything?

"Very badly," Meredith said. "Gina left the island without saying a word to Cal. He was devastated. She didn't say anything to me, either, though we quickly got to be friends. She did, however, speak to my aunt."

Aaah, Steve thought, gazing off to the opposite bank where graceful sprays of crimson flowers were blossoming amid the trees. The uppity Aunt Lorinda. A fearful snob like the rest of them except Cal and Meredith who were totally devoid of that defect.

"Gina told my aunt it was just a mad fling," Meredith said quietly. "It didn't look like it at the time. Anyway, Cal has never forgiven or forgotten her."

"Yet he got himself engaged to Kym Harrison?"

Meredith ran a finger down her flushed cheek. "I know. But it was a big mistake. There's always been a lot of pressure on Cal."

"His shoulders are plenty wide enough," Steve said admiringly.

She turned her face to him, surreptitiously studying his profile. Steven Lockhart was a great-looking guy, the golden eyes, the inky-black hair, the strong, regular features. He had an inherent authority to him. The Lancaster Legacy, though he'd bust anyone in the nose for saying it. "Cal thinks a lot of you, too."

"That's good," he reacted with dry amusement. "I always get the impression your dad would like to see me move on."

What could she say? *I don't know why my father is as he is?* Maybe her father had intercepted one of her stray looks in their overseer's direction. "That won't happen while Cal's around," she assured him. "Cal is running the station as you know. Dad has more or less semiretired. Cal's very happy with you. Didn't he leave you in charge?"

He turned his sleek black head to look smilingly into her eyes. "I thought *you* were?"

"Me?" She gave a bittersweet little laugh that nevertheless was music to his ears. "I'm not in charge of anything. No, that isn't true. I run the office. I do lots of things."

"Too smoothly," Steve said, unconsciously echoing Cal. "You make the job look too easy. People take the super-efficient for granted. Anyway go on. I want to hear this story. I've sensed, underneath, Cal is far from happy on the personal front."

"Who is?" she asked, suddenly serious. "Are *you* happy, Steven?"

I've been happier than I've ever been in my life since I met you.

He couldn't tell her that, instead he managed casually, "I'm happy sitting here with you. Or aren't I supposed to say that?"

She caught the metallic glint. "You've got a big chip on your shoulder, Steven Lockhart."

"I've got a big chip on *both* shoulders," he commented. "That's why I'm so well balanced. So this trip of Cal's is connected to Gina?"

"It's all about Gina. He's dead-set on bringing her home."

"What, here to Coronation?" That stopped him in his tracks. "This *is* his home."

"So they've reconciled after all this time?" he asked more quietly.

"There's more."

"Of course there's more." He picked up a pebble and sent it skittering across the ruffled surface of the water. "There's *always* more."

Meredith could still feel the shock of her brother's revelation. "Gina had a child, a little boy," she said simply. "His name is Robert, Robbie."

"And the child is Cal's," Steve finished for her.

Meredith released a pent-up breath. "Apparently he's the image of Cal at the same age, even to the green eyes. He's convinced Gina they should get married."

Steve gave a little grunt. "So marriage it will be, knowing Cal. What do your parents think?" He knew perfectly well the McKendricks still had their hopes set on Kym Harrison who was a nice enough down-to-earth person, but no match for Cal.

"They don't know anything about it as yet," Meredith told him, her tone tinged with worry. "It's going to come as an enormous shock and they don't like shocks. Cal rang me to tell me the news. Cal and I are very close."

"I know that." He picked up another pebble. He had to do something with his hands. "How do you feel about it? I mean, you have a nephew you didn't know about."

With a sigh she fell back against the sand, looking up at the luminous sky that was filling with birds homing into their nests. "And I can't wait to meet him. It will be wonderful to have a little nephew to love. I want to love Gina, too. I know Cal has never stopped loving her. Cal feels very deeply. I could tell he was shocked out of his mind to find he had a son but I could hear the joy, as well. This is what he truly wants."

Steve put a hand to his head, painfully aware of the length of her slender body beside his; the swell of her breasts, the curve of her hips, her lithe thighs and long legs. He got a tight rein on his feelings. *Man, don't let go or you'll go straight to hell!* But didn't she realise the way she was lying back like that presented a danger? He felt he was teetering on the brink. Relaxed around women, he was like a cat on a hot tin roof with Meredith. To counteract it he said almost sternly, "Why didn't she tell him? I can't see Cal turning his back on her, or his child!" The likes of Lancaster certainly, but not Cal McKendrick. "I don't think I could forgive a woman for doing that to me. Just think what he's missed out on. The boy must be…three?"

"They'll have to work it out, Steven," she said, and her voice wobbled a little. "Gina is from a migrant family. Italian. They had a sugar farm in North Queensland. Her heritage shows. She's very beautiful."

"More beautiful than you?" Now, why the hell had he said that? He never got too personal. It was taboo.

"Most certainly," she said, flashes of excitement heating her body. She was deeply attracted to Steven Lockhart. She'd known that for a long time. Just as she knew his prime concern had to be survival. At twenty-eight he'd made overseer on one of the nation's premier beef-producing stations, which was no mean feat. He was well paid, lots of perks. He had a future, providing he didn't get on the wrong side of her father. An adverse word from Ewan McKendrick could harm him in the industry. There was *no* future as Gavin Lancaster's illegitimate son. Lancaster refused to acknowledge him.

She shut her eyes, so now Steve was free to look down at her beautiful face. She had lovely clear skin, with a healthy gloss to it. He loved the soft dimple in her chin. He loved her finely cut mouth. He wanted to kiss it. *So badly.* He wanted to pull her long thick hair out of its plait. He wanted to arrange it the way he had often imagined himself arranging it around her face. "Don't you want to hear you're beautiful?" he asked, unable to keep some of the spiralling sensuality out of his voice.

Meredith's dark blue eyes flew open. The very air was trembling.

"Not from *you*, Steven," she said, swift and low.

He pulled back. Looked away. "Right! I get it. I'm out of line." Some part of him wanted to teach her a lesson. One she wouldn't forget. He wanted to reach for her and haul her into his arms. He could feel the dark force in him, the driving male need. Managed to get it under control, but hell, did it have some power!

"I'm not sure you *do* get it," she said, swinging up into a sitting position. "I didn't mean to offend you, Steven. I know that came out badly. I'm sorry. We're rarely alone together. I'm nervous. What I was trying to say is, *we* can't go anywhere."

His golden eyes had sparkles of light in them. "I didn't think we could, actually," he returned, his tone as cutting as a blade.

She put out a shaking, conciliatory hand; let it hover. She was frightened to touch him. She was frightened what touching him might do to her. She could see the lick of sweat on his darkly tanned skin. She wanted to put her tongue to it. "I've hurt you."

"*Never,* I hope." He flashed her an upbraiding look. "Relax, Meredith. I've put the man back in the box. I'm the dumb employee again So when are they arriving?" Crisply, he changed the subject.

The snap in his voice stung. "Cal is coming home Saturday. Gina and Robbie will follow at a later date."

And the Duke and Duchess didn't know? Only Cal McKendrick could pull that off.

"Well, I hope with all my heart it comes off." And he meant it. Cal McKendrick was not only his boss but a good friend, a supporter.

"That's very nice of you, Steven," she said softly, feeling, inexplicably about to cry. And she *never* cried. She had learned early not to.

"I'm a sweet guy," he said with an ironic twist to his truly sexy mouth.

"No, you're not." A little laugh escaped her. "You're a good person but that's not the same thing. You're a very complex man. You're carrying a lot of baggage."

"And you're not?" His black brows shot up in challenge. "Now, aren't I being outspoken today?" Extreme sarcasm charged his expression.

She stared back at him, wanting for a long time to know all about his life, aware of his deep reserve. "It must have been tough for you growing up?" she asked gently. "When did you find out about Lancaster?" The question should come as no surprise. Everyone knew the story.

He was silent for so long she didn't think he was going to answer. "I'm sorry if I'm intruding on a private grief. You don't want to talk about it?"

"I'm surprised you want to hear," he said, his mind spinning, as all of a sudden picturing himself having a child with her.

"No, you're not!" She surprised him by saying. "You know I want to hear. I like you, Steven."

"How very gracious of you, Ms McKendrick." He didn't hold the sarcasm back.

"Does it help to mock me?" she asked, turning her eyes on him.

"It does actually." He shrugged. "The difficulties of our situation and so forth. To answer your question I found out that Lancaster had fathered me when I was around ten. The man I thought was my father, Jim Lockhart, had always been a bit uncertain of me. My mother explained away my colouring as being on her side of the family. She was a honey-blond. I was the black crow among all the white feathered cockatoos. Lancaster, strangely no great womaniser, took a fancy to my mother—she was, probably still is, a very pretty woman. She said he raped her." He laughed harshly. "You can bet your life it was a lie. That was just a story to serve up to poor old Jim. Even he wasn't fooled. Lancaster didn't have to rape any woman. He could have any woman he wanted. Mum loved Jim, the father of three of her children. But sleeping with Lancaster was like sleeping with a god. A wicked one at that. She wasn't supposed to get pregnant."

"But it happened."

"It must have. *I'm* here. I'm so much like him we don't need any DNA. They took off for New Zealand where Lockhart had family. I hear from them from time to time. Jim could never take to me, especially after, but he did his best."

"So when was this? When were you on your own?" Sadness jolted her heart.

"Fourteen. I couldn't go with them, too difficult for Jim my mother explained, too destructive to the marriage. I was sent to boarding school for the next three years. They must have had to dig deep. It was a top school. My friends came from Outback properties all over Queensland. That's how I finished up as a station hand."

"Who very quickly rose to the top," she reminded him. "Have you ever spoken a word to Lancaster?"

"I couldn't trust myself to speak to him," Steve said, tasting violent anger at the back of his throat. "I despise the man. He's supposed to be Gavin Lancaster, the big man, the cattle baron! He's a spineless, gutless, wimp. One day we're going to come face-to-face. One day—"

He broke off, his expression so dark, Meredith caught a glimpse of his inner demons. "You don't need him, Steven. You're going to make your mark on your own."

"I intend to," he said. Somehow he knew he was capable of extraordinary things. "You know I've got half brothers everywhere. A Lancaster, two Lockhart's. A half sister—she was a sweet little thing—yet I feel connected to no one. Cal comes the closest."

Meredith's tender heart smote her. She saw in her mind's eye a vision of the fourteen-year-old left all alone while his family started a fresh life in another country. "Give me your hand," she said very gently, reaching out to him.

His tall, powerful body went taut. "I don't think that's a good idea," he warned, knuckles clenched white, obviously agitated when he was usually so in command.

"I want you to think of me as your friend." It seemed very important to her he did. "*Please,* Steven. I told you. I like you. I…"

She never got to finish that hopelessly inadequate sentence. With an explosive oath, he lifted her forcibly, effortlessly into his arms, so she was lying across his chest, staring up into a face brilliant with a passion he couldn't control.

"You can't try the teasing, Meredith. Not with me, you can't!"

Teasing? She had no thought of teasing in her head. "But, Steven, it's not like that!" She was so agitated she had difficulty speaking.

"Then you should be more careful," he rasped, lowering his head with such a look of hunger it overwhelmed her. Heartbeats shook her body. She was aware of an acute sense of trepidation. She had imagined something like this happening, though she had held it a secret deep within her. What if the reality fell far short of those imaginings? What if…

He kissed her until she was swooning in his arms, the excitement breathtaking. His beard was slightly rough against her soft skin, grazing it, yet it was so wonderful! He was cradling her, covering her face and neck with kisses, as if only she could make his hunger and pain go away. His hands closed around her face as he kept re-

urning to her yielding mouth, over and over, his tongue slipping
around the moist interior, exploring it and the shape of her teeth.

It was astonishing as though it were all happening in the most
voluptuous slow motion. Meredith didn't see how it could go on
without their shedding their clothes, rolling naked on the sand.
Her shirt was already off one shoulder. She was crushed against
him, the pressure of her breasts against the hard wall of his chest,
going along with this tumultuous tide, with not a thought in her
head of fighting it. She could smell him, the wonderful male
scent of him, something *warm* and intoxicating like the smell of
fine leather and warm spices.

"Do you know how beautiful you are?" he muttered. "No, stay
there." He had unloosened her thick plait, now her hair was swirling
all around them releasing the herbal scents of her shampoo. He
took a handful of it, kissed a lock, then her cheek, inhaling her skin.
She'd been working all day yet she was so fresh. Always was.

Meredith had never felt so weak in her life. Her body had
turned boneless. She didn't think she could possibly stand up or
find her balance if she did. She was making no attempt to block
his moving hands. She didn't want to. It was all too thrilling. Now
his hand was reaching into the neck of her shirt, moving down
to her breast; long strong fingers reaching further down, seeking
the nipple, already erect.

How could she stand it? She was unravelling like a bolt of silk.
She had to do something. God, what? This was *ecstasy*. She'd
had little of that. She wasn't a virgin—a few, mostly pleasant
experiences—but she'd never known anything like this or felt so
remotely close to someone. And they were only kissing. *Only!*
His fingers had reached her nipple, stimulating it further, setting
her off wildly. Sensation was spreading down to her groin. She
had to squeeze her legs together, when she wanted to throw them
wide apart. Her heart was pumping madly She didn't know it but

her nails were sinking into his back. Stars exploded behind her tightly shut eyelids, a kaleidoscope of colours.

Easier to put out a fire before it reaches a conflagration.

The warning voice in her head tried to call a stop, but she was too caught up in sensation. Calling a halt was so totally against her desire.

Meredith, you're losing yourself. Stop now. The voice came again. This time it had the power of a scream! She could so easily fall pregnant. It was a long time since she had taken the Pill.

Somehow she stayed his hand, though the effort nearly split her open. "*Please,* Steven." Her voice was no more than a ragged sob.

For a moment, an eternity, she thought he couldn't or wouldn't heed her plea. She was unsurprised. She should never have let him go so far. But, oh, it was ravishing, electric! And she had learned a few things about herself she had never known. She was electric only for *him.*

Steve's anguished groan came from way down deep in his throat. How was he supposed to let go of her after that? Didn't women understand a man couldn't just shut down at the flick of a switch? He didn't know how to protect himself from the pain. He buried his face in her sweetly scented neck, his hands breaking off caressing her. He could have howled aloud. "I don't know what to say," he muttered, as much to himself as her.

"You don't have to say anything," she tried to comfort him, feeling as if they were sealed off from the rest of the world.

"I frightened you for a moment, didn't I?" He threw his head back to stare into her eyes, his own glowing.

"Maybe," she whispered, not hiding from the truth. "I frightened myself, too."

He gave a strange laugh. "See what happens when you ask to hold my hand?"

"It's been coming a long time. But you know what they say? Forewarned, is forearmed." She tried to joke, when she had never felt so emotional, allowing her forehead to rest against his. "I care about you, Steven. I don't simply like you. I really care."

He accepted that now. All that wild passion wasn't only on his side. The tremors that shook her had been real. For long moments there he had thought she would let him do anything he liked with her. Let him peel off her clothes, run his tongue over every inch of her satiny body, find every little secret crevice. "If someone saw us and reported to your dad I'd be out of here this same afternoon," he said wryly, thinking it would have been well worth it. "Even Cal couldn't save me."

She felt bolder, stronger, than she had ever felt in her life. "*I'd* save you," she said, planting a kiss near the corner of his eye. "My father has played the heavy in too many of my relationships. God knows why. It's a puzzle. Cal is the one my parents love and adore. Not me."

"They must be mad," he muttered thickly and with disgust. "A wonderful daughter like you to fill their lives?"

She gave him another sweet kiss, this time on the cheek. "I must get up. Go home, Steven." Life went on. Reality replaced rapture. She had to make a big decision. She had to decide what she really wanted out of life. She had to decide if the emotion that had ripped through her like a hurricane could move on from a powerful sexual attraction to something deeper, stronger, more permanent. She realised she expected it with a man like Steven Lockhart. There were deep waters beneath that calm, controlled exterior, deep surging passions.

A kiss can be life changing. Strange but true.

With her hair undone it was blowing this way and that in the late-afternoon breeze. "You've wrecked my hair," she said, smiling down at him, the warm flush in her cheeks highlighting the burning blue of her eyes.

"You wouldn't say that if you could see yourself. A woman's hair truly is her crowning glory." He sat looking at her, his heart ravished, as she rebuttoned her shirt, then set about re-plaiting the gleaming masses. "How is it going to be from now on, Meredith?" he asked, his tone very serious. "I couldn't have made it more obvious how I feel about you. Now everything has changed. How do we handle that?"

She flicked her thick plait over her shoulder, making the decision to speak the truth. "I want…I want *you,* Steven."

He nodded as though she had revealed something very important. Then, "Talk around the station is, your parents want you to marry that McDermott guy. Are you going to do it?"

She began to brush sand off her clothes. "Nope."

"He's got a lot to offer," he persisted. The McDermotts were a wealthy pastoral family and McDermott was a likeable guy, a great polo player.

"I suppose. Everything but love." She didn't tell him Shane McDermott had already proposed to her. Twice.

"So where are you leading me, Heaven, or Hell?" He stood up; looming over her, a superbly fit young man, his golden-brown eyes searching her face.

"What about the stars?" she suggested softly, wishing the two of them could stay like this for ever.

"I'd snatch them down for you if I could." He pulled her tight…tighter.

"I'll remember that." She leaned back against his arm.

They stayed like that for long moments staring into one another's eyes, then he released her. She turned away to pick up her hat, settling it jauntily on her head. It was very difficult trying to return to normal again. Steven was right. Every second of their explosive lovemaking had brought them closer and closer to-gether. Everything had, indeed, changed. Her desires, her long-ings, her hopes had been dredged up from some deep quarry inside her. She had to start thinking about wanting *more* instead of settling into a pattern of accepting *less*.

"Let's move slowly," she said, blue eyes going back to him, seeking his understanding. "One day at a time." She knew op-position from her parents would be fierce if she came out with her feelings for Steven Lockhart. "Okay?" She sought some ges-ture of agreement. "I don't care if we're seen together often. I'm past pretence." She waited nervously for his answer, frightened he might move back from the brink, seeing himself as a man with a lot to lose and probably nothing to win.

He inclined his raven head. "Whatever you say." How he wished he had more to offer her. Right *now*. He knew he could get it, but it would take time. "I guess your family will have enough on its hands welcoming Gina and their little grandson."

She sighed in agreement. "You'll be hearing about it." She held his gaze, wanting to make sure he understood the opened lines of communication between them really mattered. Changes came through making decisions and carrying them through. If she wanted Steven Lockhart—and she realised she did—she knew she would have to give up her ingrained reticence and *reach* for him. He had suffered too much rejection and he was a man of pride.

To her relief he gave her a little salute. "At the end of the day, this is going to affect us all."

It was only after she rode away that the voice in his head be-gan. It whispered words of caution that dropped, heavy as a pile of stones.

Remember who she is, Steve.

Yet she had come willingly and without resistance into his

arms. She was as powerfully attracted to him as he was to her. That much he knew. Or had they both simply surrendered to an overwhelming temptation? And what about the McKendrick rules? Cal had broken them. Even for him it hadn't been simple. How much more difficult for Meredith?

When Meredith went downstairs some fifteen minutes before dinner—which was always at 7:00 p.m. on the dot, dress please, no jeans, slacking not accepted—her mother called to her the moment she saw her.

"There you are, dear," Jocelyn spoke brightly. "Join me for a moment, would you?" She beckoned Meredith to follow her down to the library, leaving behind her a light trail of her very expensive signature perfume.

"Anything wrong, Mum?" Meredith asked when they were inside the room. It was huge, but wonderfully atmospheric and welcoming despite the size. She loved books. Couldn't live without them. For years she had wanted to make a start on cataloguing the library—Uncle Ed had been keen to join her—but they both realised they were going to be refused the project.

Don't bother me now, Meredith. When I decide the time's right I'll call in a professional. Someone who knows what he's about.

He. That was her father, the quintessential chauvinist.

The ambience of the library settled her slightly when, truth be known, she was a bundle of nerves what with Cal's affairs and hers. Cal couldn't come home soon enough so far as his sister was concerned.

Jocelyn turned about, delicate brows raised like wings. "Why should anything be wrong, dear? No, no, I was planning on asking Kym to stay for the week-end." She settled herself gracefully into a deep comfortable chair, upholstered in a rich paisley, indicating to Meredith to take the one opposite. "I thought you might like to ask Shane. Make up a foursome." She gave her daughter an encouraging smile. "You're getting on, my dear. Time to settle down. One should have one's children young. Your father and I did."

"I'm not twenty-six yet, Mum," Meredith said thinking subtlety often eluded her mother.

"Twenty-six is getting on," Jocelyn said, her voice firm.

"Not what anyone else would call over the hill," Meredith murmured dryly. "And aren't you forgetting something, Mum?"

"Remind me." She put a hand to her triple string of large, lustrous pearls. She was rarely seen without them even if they were half hidden by collars or under sweaters and the like. They were a wedding present from her husband and very valuable.

"Dad has made an art form of scaring off my admirers," Meredith pointed out. As if her mother didn't know! And often condoned.

"Don't be ridiculous!" Jocelyn now studied her slim ankles. She had kept her tiny waist and youthful figure and was very proud of it. "Only the fortune hunters, dear. Shane isn't one of those."

"No, indeed, he's *one of us,*" Meredith lightly mocked, thinking in some respects her mother was a throwback to far less egalitarian times. "Shane and I aren't going anywhere, Mum. Sorry to disappoint you. I like him. I value him as a friend, but I'm not and never will be in love with him."

Jocelyn's equable temper suddenly flared, putting diamond chips into her glass-green eyes. Jocelyn thoroughly disliked having her plans thwarted. "Who said anything about love?" she demanded to know. "There are far more important things than love in a marriage, my girl. Love can fly out the window as fast as it flew in. You have to consider more lasting qualities. Similar backgrounds, shared interests, liking and respect. Friendship is very important. Friendship between the families, as well. I'd like you to know—"

"Did you love Dad when you married him?" Meredith interrupted the flow, wondering if her authoritarian father had ever been a lovable person.

Jocelyn did effrontery exceedingly well. "Of course I loved your father. How could you ask? We are *still* in love."

Meredith supposed they were in their own way.

"And we're excellent friends. Your father and I see eye to eye. We've been greatly blessed. We have our wonderful son. A better son no parent could ask for. And we have you. You're a beautiful young woman, Meredith. Or you could be if you ever decided to do something about yourself. You could take a leaf out of Kym's book there. She's always marvellously turned out. All I ever see you in is jeans with your hair scraped back. It's scraped back even now."

Meredith put a hand to the loose curls that lay along her cheeks. "And here I was thinking I had prettied it up. Could the fact I do a lot of work around the station, as well as in the office have anything to do with the way I dress, do you suppose? It might come as a surprise to you, but Kym has often told me she'd give anything to look as good as I do in jeans."

Jocelyn lifted a porcelain ornament—eighteenth-century Meissen—off the small circular table beside her, then put it down again gently. "Well, she is a bit pear shaped," she conceded with a smile. "So what about it? We ask them both, Kym and Shane. Give the poor boy a chance, dear. You won't have any trouble with your father. I've already spoken to him. We like Shane."

Meredith clasped her hands together. Looking down at them she was sure she should be taking more care of them. Especially now when she had never felt more a woman. Bring on the hand cream! "Be that as it may, Mum, you're wasting your time. I don't think this week-end is a good time to invite anyone. Cal won't want to come home to find Kym here. Do you never stop hoping?" Meredith looked at her mother with pitying eyes.

Jocelyn had gone through life getting what she wanted. Maybe that was why she couldn't seem to give up on Kym. After all, she and Beth Harrison had dreamed of a marriage, uniting the two families and eventually uniting the two stations.

"Never!" Jocelyn gave a shake of her beautifully groomed head, dark hair swept back off a high brow. "Kym suits Cal perfectly."

"Kym suits *you* perfectly, Mum," Meredith corrected. "There's a big difference. The engagement didn't work. It's never going to work. Please don't ask Kym over. It won't be any nice surprise for Cal, believe me. He may have a few surprises of his own."

Jocelyn, who had settled back, sat up straight, her unlined forehead suddenly furrowed. "Meaning what? Are you trying to tell me something, Meredith? If you are, I'd advise you to be out with it. You surely can't be inferring Cal has someone hidden away?" She looked aghast at the very idea.

"Why don't you wait until he comes home," Meredith advised, and went to stand hesitantly by her mother.

"What is it, Meredith?" Jocelyn looked up to meet her daughter's gaze directly. "You know I hate surprises. I like to know *exactly* what's going on."

Meredith let her hand rest on her mother's shoulder. "Cal does have some news, Mum, but it's not my news to tell. He'll be home on Saturday. You'll have to be patient until then."

CHAPTER FOUR

THEY were all gathered around the long mahogany table in the formal dining room listening to Cal deliver his momentous news. It was an elaborate setting, Meredith thought. The table, for instance, had always reminded her of the deck of an aircraft carrier. Around it were ranged Georgian chairs, tied with elaborate silk tassels, convex gilded mirrors on the walls, a magnificent Dutch still life over the sideboard—fruit, vegetables, game birds. Only one of the great chandeliers was on. Even then the light was dazzling. The room was only used for gala occasions— but it seemed as good a place as any for her brother to tell his extraordinary story.

Cal told it simply, but movingly. He had to convey to them how powerfully Gina Romano had affected him from the very first moment he saw her. He had wanted no other woman. No way could he tell them in bringing Gina here he was bending her to his will. He had to stick to the charade. He must have been convincing, because Meredith's expression was soft and tender. She looked thrilled.

And thrilled Meredith was. If Steven could feel the same way about her as Cal did about his Gina, what a priceless gift that would be! The rest of the family greeted Cal's news with a ringing silence.

This was never meant to happen!

Meredith's eyes flew to her brother's, renewing her support. Still, the family continued to sit there as if they'd been turned to stone; or Cal had spoken in an unfamiliar tongue and they were struggling to decipher it. Meredith gritted her teeth, her throat aching with tension.

Their father, for once, was plainly at a loss. Nothing in response. He started to speak, then stopped. Their mother held her fingers to her temples as though she had suddenly developed an appalling headache, which, indeed, she had. Uncle Ed continued to stare down at the gleaming surface of the table as though amazed at the shine.

"I don't believe this," Jocelyn finally burst out, in evident anger and confusion. It tore at her, making her blind to anyone else's feelings but her own. "This is the most appalling news. This Gina doesn't sound the sort of girl you would bring home. Let alone *marry.*"

Meredith winced, hardly daring to look at her brother to gauge his reaction. "Mum, *please!*" she begged, excruciatingly embarrassed by her mother's outburst.

Jocelyn ignored her, beginning to cry, but Cal's handsome features showed no softening. They hardened to granite. He thrust back his chair and then stood up, addressing his mother. "How did you get to be such an appalling snob, Mother?" he asked, his voice tight. "I'm sure the Queen of England wouldn't carry on like you. You've gone on with your PLU nonsense ever since I can remember. There has to be an end to it."

He sounded so disgusted that Jocelyn, who was used to the greatest respect from her son, started to pull herself together. "Lorinda did warn me," she said, in that moment of stress letting the cat out of the bag. "She was most concerned."

Cal's heart tightened up like a fist. "When was this?"

Jocelyn didn't answer. Instead she made a small agitated flourish with her hand.

"Are you saying you knew back then?" Suddenly Cal had to confront the fact Lorinda, the aunt he had always trusted, had deceived him.

"Of course we knew, son." Ewan McKendrick reached out to take his wife's shaking hand. "And she had your child?" The question ended upwards in a kind of wonderment.

"Your grandson, Dad," Cal told him, strong emotions etched on his face. "It's just as I told you. I never knew."

"I'm certain you didn't," Ewan responded on the instant. "You're a man of honour."

"Honour short of *marriage,* you mean, Dad?" Cal asked bitterly. "Provide for her and the boy. Sweep it under the carpet. Get on with life. I'm afraid that's not on. I'm going to marry Gina. I'm going to bring her and my son home."

Jocelyn blew her nose exceedingly hard when she was always so dainty about such things. "But how can you love her after all she's done to you?" she cried. "She's a heartless woman. Not worth knowing. You probably wouldn't look at her now," she added, though it didn't make a lot of sense.

Meredith rushed to support her brother. "Gina is a beautiful person, Mum. Anyone would be proud to welcome her into the family."

Jocelyn burst into fresh tears. She had no desire whatever to meet this Gina person. But Gina's son? That was a matter of great concern to her. The boy was Cal's heir.

"Let me repeat I'm going to bring Gina and our son home." Cal didn't know it but he looked colder and harder than his father ever had.

"And is he going to be page boy at the wedding?" Jocelyn stopped her tears, to enquire with great sarcasm. "Where is this wedding going to be held, may I ask? Not here. I won't be humiliated in front of the world. I couldn't bear it." She followed up that announcement with an exaggerated shudder.

"Steady on, Jocelyn." Ewan held up a warning hand. He knew his son if Jocelyn didn't. No way could he allow his son to take leave of the family. Ewan knew Cal would, if pushed.

"What do you think, Uncle Ed?" Cal looked across the table at his uncle who had remained silent throughout as though being seen was one thing, heard another. Not that anyone could get a word in with Jocelyn.

Ed spread his hands. His sister-in-law was behaving in a disastrous fashion but he was living in the family home. Hell, he had a right to it come to that! "Anything that makes you happy, makes me happy, Cal." He said with obvious sincerity. "I'm sure your Gina is as beautiful as Merri says. I can see you're stunned, but your mother and Lorinda have always been as thick as thieves."

Jocelyn gasped. "Shame, shame, shame, Ed McKendrick. Lorinda is a loyal sister and she *adores* Cal," she rebuked him. "Lorinda acted on the highest motivation, love and concern. It was your Gina who ran off, Cal, back to her own world. Is that how to love someone, deceiving them then running away? Utterly spineless I say."

Cal strove to keep the fury and confusion he was feeling out of his voice. "I think the less you say, the better, Mum. This is a fait accompli. I've found the mother of my son. I'm finally going to bring them home. Her and Robert."

Jocelyn's green eyes gushed afresh. "Damn it, damn it, damn it!" she cried, her whole body trembling under the force of her shock and anger. "No wonder you didn't want Kym over, Meredith." She turned on her daughter as though she were greatly to blame. "Kym will be devastated when she hears about this."

"For God's sake, my dear, you're flogging a dead horse,"

Ewan McKendrick groaned, raising a hand to stay his wife. "I have told you."

Jocelyn stared back at her husband, feeling greatly undermined. "The point is *you* wanted Kym, too, Ewan. She was *our* choice. Not some young woman who won't belong. Had Cal and Kym married, in time Lakefield would have been added to the McKendrick chain. It was all so suitable."

"Business is business and PLU is PLU, eh, Mum?" Meredith couldn't resist the dig.

Her father turned cold blue eyes on her. "Please don't speak to your mother like that, Meredith."

"I'm only stating an evident truth, Dad. Why don't you stop treating me like a child?"

Jocelyn broke in irritably. "I don't think I'll ever forgive you for not warning me, Meredith. I've suffered a betrayal. I'm terribly, terribly wounded."

"Then I'm sorry, Mum. But as I pointed out at the time, it was Cal's story to tell."

"Exactly! I told Meredith to leave it to me," Cal confirmed in a clipped voice.

"What, keep the truth from me, Calvin?" Jocelyn asked piteously.

Ewan wasn't attending to anything being said. "I haven't met my grandson and he's three years of age," he murmured, very poignantly for him. "Who does he look like?" He turned beseeching eyes on his son.

Cal sat down again, sighing heavily. "Like you, Dad, like me. He's a McKendrick, but he has Mum's green eyes."

"My green eyes!" Jocelyn spluttered, as though only one other person in the world was entitled to them. "You're the one with my green eyes, Calvin. It's impossible, I tell you. She can't come here." Jocelyn's small face started to crease up again. "I won't be grooming a total stranger, to take over from me. Not that she could," she added scathingly. She stared back at her son. No adoration there, only anger and condemnation.

"If Gina isn't welcome here, *I* don't stay." Cal laid down the ultimatum, looking grimly resolute.

There was no question in at least three people's minds he meant it. "I can wait it out until it's my time to inherit. You don't own Coronation Hill, Dad. You're the custodian. Just as I will be for *my* son, my son Robert."

But Ewan McKendrick was way ahead of them all. "As though I would ask you to go," he cried, exhibiting great dismay, and not looking at his wife. "When is it you want to bring Gina and the boy home?"

Oh, thank God, thank God! Meredith gave silent praises. When the chips were down, their father always chose the smartest course.

Cal shot a wry glance at his sister, reading her mind. "By the end of this month. This house is big enough to swallow up the lot of us. We wouldn't have to see one another if we didn't want to," he added satirically, though it was perfectly true.

"Good God, son, we don't want you to go into hiding!" Ewan exclaimed. "Dear me, no. What's happened, has happened. Now we must move forward. The sooner the better."

"Thanks for that, Dad," Cal said, the severe tension in him easing fractionally. "In view of what I've just heard I need to have a talk with Aunt Lorinda." Anger and disillusionment flinted from his brilliant eyes.

"Well, you'll just have to wait now, won't you!" Jocelyn cried in a kind of triumph. "She's in Europe."

"She'll be back," Cal answered shortly. It was important he get to the bottom of the matter. Gina hadn't said anything that implicated Lorinda in her decision to flee the island, but the fact his aunt and his mother had discussed their blossoming romance had suddenly opened up a Pandora's Box.

"So when do you plan to take your marriage vows?" Ewan was asking, busy looking at the situation from all its angles in his head. Wouldn't even make a nine day wonder he shouldn't be surprised. Times had changed dramatically, if only Jocelyn could see it!

"I'm not entirely sure." Cal glanced across at his sister. What better sister could a man have? Yet he couldn't tell her Gina wasn't exactly ecstatic about marrying him. He was forcing her into it. He wasn't happy about that, but he was determined on his course. Robert was a McKendrick. His place was on Coronation Hill. Robert needed his parents together, not apart, two people to love and raise him. He couldn't risk Gina marrying someone else, providing an alternative father to *his* son.

"If you're going to go ahead with this it will be better if you marry her at some register office. Brisbane, Sydney, Adelaide, whatever," Jocelyn said bitterly. "I'm sure your sister will be delighted to act as a witness."

"Absolutely! I'd be honoured," Meredith said. "I think it's a miracle Cal and Gina have come together again."

"With *your* help!" Jocelyn bitterly accused her daughter, so often the scapegoat.

"No register office," Ewan broke in, his stern glance silencing his daughter who was about to respond to her mother. "The wedding will be here on Coronation."

Jocelyn looked at her husband with betrayal in her reddened eyes. "You can't mean it, Ewan."

"All the McKendricks have been married from here," he answered, with blunt force. "Including you, Ed. We've all had huge weddings, great celebrations. We're going to do things right."

"And if I refuse to be here?" Jocelyn threw down the challenge.

Ewan reached out to pat her shoulder. "But you won't refuse, will you, my dear? You've always been an excellent wife." He turned his arrogant, handsome head towards his son. "Would you like that, Cal?"

"That's what I want, Dad," Cal said. "But nothing big."

"Frankly I don't see how we can avoid it." For the first time Ewan smiled. "You've been through a tough time."

"*Gina* has been through a tough time," Cal said, mustering up his most caring tone.

"That's absurd." His mother might have seen through him she gave such a scoffing laugh.

"She must be a strong person." Ewan cut in, frowning on his wife. Ewan McKendrick was every inch the diplomat whenever an occasion demanding diplomacy arose. "Bring Gina home, son. We'll make her welcome." He ignored his wife's bitter exclamation, but turned on her a rare, cold eye. "I can't wait to meet my grandson. Especially if he looks like me."

Would a little granddaughter have fared so well, I wonder? Meredith thought, then immediately chided herself for being so mean.

"Thank God that's over," she said an hour later, after she and Cal made their escape to the garden. "It was a bit of a surprise learning Aunt Lorinda was busy informing Mum of everything that went on at the island. Do you suppose she had anything to do with Gina's abrupt departure? Now that I think about it, I wouldn't put it past her, though she was always sweet to Gina."

"Yes, she was." Cal was forced to admit it, but inside he was hurting badly. He had blamed Gina for years, when it now seemed he didn't know the full story.

"Gina didn't explain why she left?" Meredith read his mind.

"She certainly didn't say Lorinda made any decision for her."

"So what was Gina's decision based on?" Meredith frowned. "Wouldn't she say?"

Cal stared up at the brilliant clusters of stars. "Merri, Gina made it quite plain she wants to shut the door on the past. She refused to get into any discussion, but I gathered she thought at the time she wasn't good enough for me. Pretty damned silly, I know. But I suppose looking at it from her side she was made aware there was plenty of money being splashed around. She came from an ordinary family with I imagine little money to spare on luxury holidays. Perhaps she felt overwhelmed. People do. You know that."

"But Gina gave no sign of it," Meredith said. "Her manner couldn't have been more natural. Gina could take her place any-where."

"She was so *young*," Cal said. "Maybe that accounts for it. She got frightened off."

"Did you ever mention Kym to her?" Meredith persisted. "The fact Mum and Dad cherished hopes the two of you would marry?"

"God, no!" Cal protested violently. "I never gave Kym a thought. There was only Gina. But she found out later about Kym. She saw a photo of us in some magazine. Kym and I were engaged at the time."

"Oh!" Meredith gave a little anguished moan. "Do you sup-pose Aunt Lorinda might have told her about Kym? She saw a grand love affair unfolding right under her nose. Time to put a stop to it. We now know she contacted Mum."

"I'll get to the bottom of it, don't you worry," Cal said with quiet menace. "Gina had her opportunity to denounce Lorinda. If there was anything to denounce. She didn't."

Meredith pondered it all in silence. "So what happened to Gina's boyfriend? I imagine the marriage was well and truly off when Gina discovered she was pregnant?"

"Now *that's* the strange thing. Gina claims there was no boy-friend," Cal answered. "She must have gone into denial. I'm fairly sure she was frightened of her father. He's dead, by the way." He held back a curling palm frond from his sister's face. "Did you get around to telling Steve any of this?"

She nodded, grateful for the cloak of darkness. "You said I could. He was very sympathetic. Steve's on your side. He's had a hard life. He understands a great deal."

"You like him, don't you?" Cal spoke directly.

She felt the heat rush into her skin. "I do." Meredith was beyond pretence. She had to get a life. "He's quite a guy. But can you imagine if *I'd* told Mum and Dad tonight I was preg-nant and Steve was the father, what their reaction would have been? Krakatoa! Do you really think Dad would have jumped in to say we must be married on Coronation? The crazy ironies of life, brother. We live by a different set of rules."

"They're not *my* rules, Merri," Cal said, with the greatest regret, knowing her assertion to be true. "Dad and Mum—es-pecially Mum—have to lighten up." He broke off to stare down at her. "Say, you're not telling me in a roundabout way you *are* pregnant?"

"What would be your reaction?" she asked, confident she knew what it would be.

They kept walking. "If he loved you and you loved him I could only be happy for you, Merri. Love is all that matters."

"Tell that to Mum," Meredith replied. "No, I'm not pregnant, though Mum has recently told me I'm leaving it almost too late to have kids. She wanted to invite Shane over this weekend. Shane *and* Kym."

"Struth!" Cal exclaimed wryly. "I just hope Mum hasn't been giving Kym false encouragement. That would be too cruel."

"I don't think Kym needed anyone's encouragement,"

Meredith said. "I think she has just been waiting for you to come to your senses as it were."

"Some people are just one-track. I'm sorry if Mum's going to take it out on you, Merri. It's too bad the way she does that."

"It does tend to fray the nerves," Meredith admitted, "but I'm here for you, brother." She tucked her arm through his, as though anchoring him to the moment.

"And I'm here for you, Merri. Never forget that."

Gina didn't put her apartment on the market. There was no way she could tell if a marriage between herself and Cal would work out. But what real alternative did she have but to try? There was no way she could risk not having her beloved Robbie with her all the time. A custody battle would be costly, time-consuming and in the end she would be the loser, forced into, at best, sharing custody with Robbie's father and his family, all locked away in their private stronghold. No wonder she had simply folded like a pack of cards.

She didn't dare look deep inside her heart. Except sometimes at night.

"You're still in love with him. You are and always will be."

Always the inner voice to never let her escape.

Cal McKendrick was and remained her incurable addiction. Maybe they would have a chance if he were an ordinary man, a colleague like Nat Goldman. She had met Nat's family. They would have been delighted if the friendship between her and Nat had become more serious. She remembered Cal's beautiful sister, Meredith, on the island. Meredith had always been so friendly yet she had the sense there was a considerable gulf between them. Such wealth as the McKendrick family had, was quite outside her experience. She had never witnessed anything like it. She hadn't started the affair with Cal. An affair had never occurred to her. She had been too much aware of her position on the island to offer any male guest the slightest encouragement, let alone *him*. She had been hired as a domestic/waitress, whatever was needed. She certainly needed the money to help her through her final semester. She was the first in her family ever to attend university. That in itself had been a great source of pride to her father. She had scored the highest rating. At university she had once been voted the girl with the three *B*'s. Brilliance. Beauty. Brains. Just a fun thing. No one had mentioned anything about Luck.

Her family had had little money to spare, however hard her father had toiled. Theirs had been a small sugar farm not a plantation. There was no way she would have embarked on what in the end turned out to be the most momentous, the most unforgettable, the most painful course of her life.

Cal McKendrick had been her lost love.

Until now.

When she told Rosa about Cal's re-entry into her life, Rosa had barely been able to contain herself.

"What's he want this time?" she asked, her voice, as always, fiercely protective.

Even Rosa had been silenced when Gina told her what Cal McKendrick wanted was marriage.

"You still love him?"

"I can't help it." No point in covering up from Rosa. Rosa would see through it.

"Gran Dio!" In response, Rosa balled up a rock melon and pitched it through the open kitchen window into the backyard where it narrowly missed a visiting cat who took off shrieking for safer territory. "Tell him I come with you for a week or so, perhaps a month. We face this family together. You and Roberto are *my* family. I am Aunt Rosa. You cannot do without my support."

When Cal phoned, Gina passed on Rosa's message, which was more or less an ultimatum. If she had expected some kind of sarcastic comment, even downright opposition, he had only laughed. "That's nice!" Cal phoned often. Probably checking on her whereabouts, if he didn't already have someone on the job. She had even started to check if there were any strange cars parked for any length of time in front of her apartment block. No way was she going to be allowed to abscond with his son.

Then there was Robbie. She had spent a good deal of time pondering what she would tell him, but if she had agonised over what to say: that the man Robbie had met only a short while ago, the man he had taken such a liking to, was in reality, his father, Robbie wonder of wonders took it near effortlessly on board.

"He's my daddy?" he asked, his eyes full of amazement and a dawning delight. "Where is he right now?"

"Are you listening to me, Robbie? Cal's your *father*." She hadn't expected it to be this easy. She was worried he didn't fully understand. Bright as he was he was still very young.

"Yes, Mummy." Robbie replied blithely, "but where *is* he?"

She had swallowed the hard knot in her throat. "He's back home, Robbie. His family is what is known as cattle barons. That means they own vast properties in the Outback they call *stations*."

"Like train stations?" Robbie nodded knowledgeably.

"No, darling. A train station is a stopping place where passengers get on and off," she explained. Robbie had never been, in fact, on a train. He had always travelled by car. "In Australia we call really huge farms with lots and lots of land, *stations*. There are cattle stations and sheep stations and sometimes sheep and cattle together. The McKendrick holdings—they have a number of what they call *outstations*—are cattle stations. You must have heard cowboys in the videos you watch call them *ranches*. That's the American word. We say stations."

"Wow! So Cal's a cowboy?" Robbie asked in such delight his greatest ambition might have been to be one.

"Well, a cattleman like he said."

"That's *wild!*" Robbie breathed. "Cal said he was going to show me some time." So at the tender age of three, Robbie was taking in his stride what might have shocked an older child or cast him into a state of panic.

"The time's almost here, Robbie," Gina said. "Your father is coming for us at the end of the month. Not long to go now. We have to leave Queensland and live in the Northern Territory. I'll show you on the map where it is. It borders Queensland, but it's a long, long way from here."

"How do we get there…by train? Gosh, I hope so." The excitement showed. "The great big long one on the TV. The Ghan, they call it. It travels through all that red desert with no one in it."

Gina shook her head. "I'm sure we'll travel on the Ghan one day but your father will be picking us up in the family plane."

Robbie's eyes went as round as saucers. "My daddy flies a plane?" Seated on a chair facing his mother he suddenly dropped to his knees, staring up at her and squeezing her hands.

"It's not a great big plane like you've seen at the airport," Gina hastened to tell him. "It's much smaller."

Robbie dramatically collapsed on the carpet. "He must be very rich!"

"Sort of." Gina didn't want to stress that side of it. "Your father and I are going to get married. How do you feel about that, my darling boy?" She gazed down earnestly into his beautiful little face.

Now all of a sudden Robbie looked deeply flustered. "I don't know. Do you *have* to?"

She couldn't begin to imagine what she would do if he suddenly burst into tears. "Your father wants us to be a family,

Robbie," she explained very gently. "I will become Mrs McKendrick. You will become Robert McKendrick. We take your father's name."

Robbie rolled onto his stomach. "It sounds very nice," he said after a few seconds of consideration. "He likes to call me Robert, doesn't he?"

"Yes, he does like I often call you Roberto. I don't want you to forget your Italian heritage. That's why Rosa and I speak Italian to you, as well as English."

Robbie gave a perky little nod. "My friend Connie speaks Italian just like me. Jonathon speaks Greek and Rani speaks Vietnamese. We think it's fun being able to speak another language."

"And so it is. So the answer's yes, Robbie?" she asked. "Your father and I will be getting married."

Robbie jumped to his feet, and then threw himself into his mother's arms. "I guess it's all right. But what is going to happen to Aunt Rosa?"

Gina silently applauded her son's caring nature. "Rosa is going to come with us." Her arms closed around her precious son, while a tear slid down her cheek. "At least for a little while to help us settle in."

"Goody, hurray!" Robbie lifted his head from her shoulder to give her a beatific smile. "I'd hate to leave Aunt Rosa behind."

"We'll never lose Aunt Rosa," Gina said.

It was a solemn promise.

CHAPTER FIVE

TEN minutes before the plane was due in, many of Coronation's considerable complement of staff began to assemble. They lined the airstrip in front of the giant hangar. This was a day of celebration. Cal was bringing his family home, the young woman soon to be his wife and their three-year-old son. Everyone had been told an aunt of Cal's fiancée was to accompany them. Whatever the lovers' star-crossed past, everything was set to be put right. A big bar-b-que had been planned for the staff starting around seven. The latest addition to the McKendrick clan would probably be tucked up in bed fast asleep, but the family was expected to look in on proceedings at some part of the evening.

Whatever Gina had expected, it wasn't a welcoming party. As they came in to land she could see all the people assembled on the ground. Even Rosa who had determined on being unimpressed, rolled her eyes and gestured with her hands. "Like something out of a movie!"

It was true. The aerial view of the great station complex was fantastic. It looked like an isolated settlement set down in the middle of a vast empty landscape that stretched away in every direction as far as the eye could see. Gina remembered reading somewhere the Northern Territory had less than one percent of the population of Texas in the U.S.A although it was twice the size. So there was a long way to go in the Territory's development. It was still frontier country and perhaps because of it wildly exciting.

She couldn't begin to count the number of buildings. The homestead had to be the building that stood apart from the rest, set within an oasis of green. It appeared to be enormous if the roof was any indication. The airstrip was at a fair distance from the homestead. It was easy to pick out from the huge hangar that had a logo painted on the silver glinting roof. It appeared to be a stylised crown. Beside the hangar stood a tall mast with the Australian flag flying from it. Farther away she could see holding yards jam-packed with cattle, three circular dams, probably bores. Beyond the complex lay the vast wilderness.

Some areas of it resembled jungle, other areas were almost parkland. Dotted all over the landscape were winding streams and smaller tributaries she supposed were the billabongs. They were quite distinct in character from the huge lagoons mostly circular and oval, where palms and pandanus grew in profusion. She could see a huge mob of horses running down there. Wild horses by the look of them, the Outback's famous brumbies.

Robbie, who had been alight with excitement at his very first plane trip, had actually slept for most of the flight. Now he was wide-awake and raring to go.

They were dropping altitude, coming in to land. Her stomach muscles clenched in anticipation, though it had been a remarkably smooth flight with Cal, a seasoned pilot, at the controls. He gave every appearance of a man who thoroughly enjoyed flying. With great distances to be covered, she began to appreciate how private aircraft in the Outback would seem more a necessity than a luxury, although she knew this particular plane cost a good deal more than one million dollars.

"Steady on, matey!" Robbie cried out in gleeful excitement, clapping his hands together. This was the adventure of a lifetime.

"Sit still now, little darling." Gina placed a calming hand on him.

"Who are all those people down there?" he asked in wonderment.

"Station staff," Gina whispered back.

That thrilled Robbie and made him laugh. More people appeared as if they had been hiding in the hangar.

"Big, *big!*" Rosa exclaimed, gesticulating with evident awe.

It was big all right!

The tyres gave a couple of gentle thumps on the tarmac, the brakes screeched, then Cal cut back to idle as they taxied towards the hangar. There he cut the engines, making his afterchecks. A few minutes later they were walking down the steps into the brilliant Territory sunlight.

"These are *our* people, Robbie," Cal explained, swooping his son high in his arms.

"Why? Are you a prince or something, Daddy?" Robbie asked, touching his father's face and staring into his eyes as though Cal was the font of all wisdom and authority. Robbie had learned all about the Queen and the royal family at nursery school. There was a picture of the Queen in a beautiful yellow dress in his old classroom. The teacher had told them a famous Australian artist called Sir William Dargie had painted it.

"A prince? No way!" Cal laughed. "I'm just an ordinary person."

That had to be the understatement of the year, Gina thought, trying to calm her own jittering nerves. Robbie had taken to calling Cal "Daddy" in the blink of an eye. No working up to it. It was as though her little son had longed to use the word. Both of them, man and boy, appeared to be going on instinct. Cal and his son had reached a place from the outset where the relationship was set. She was proud of the fact Robbie had found enormous security with her, his mother, but there was no denying the very special role of a father. It was as Cal had said. Robbie needed *both* his parents. Their son was revelling in the family wholeness.

"Other kids have a mummy and daddy. Now so do I!"

That observation had been delivered with tremendous satisfaction. Why had she ever thought him too small to notice her single-parent status?

With Rosa standing excitedly at her shoulder, Gina watched as a tall, very slender young woman—it had to be Meredith—broke ranks and rushed towards them.

"Welcome, welcome," Meredith was crying happily.

Gina was enveloped in a hug. "I've thought of you so often, Gina," Meredith said. "It's wonderful you're here."

"It's wonderful you're here to meet me." Gina was unable to prevent the emotional tears from springing to her eyes. "Meredith, I'd like you to meet my aunt Rosa. She has always been a great support to me."

"Lovely to meet you, Rosa." Meredith smiled warmly, both women taking to each other on sight. Meredith had been expecting a "motherly type" figure but Aunt Rosa was a striking, very sexy-looking woman with remarkably good skin.

"Lovely to meet *you,* my dear." Rosa well satisfied with what she saw, put her arms around Meredith and hugged her back.

Meredith turned excitedly to her brother and the little boy in his arms. "Well, I recognise *you,* young man," she said, laying a gentle, faintly trembling hand on Robbie's flushed cheek. "You're the image of your daddy." Her brilliant eyes went to her brother's. "This is truly marvellous, Cal."

His triumphant smile flashed back at her. "Isn't it just? This is your aunty Meredith, Robbie." He introduced them with pride. "I told you all about her, remember? Meredith is my sister."

"Merri," Robbie said. "You called her Merri, like Merry Christmas."

"Merri it is," Meredith said, shaking the little hand Robbie gave her. "Do you want to come and meet the rest of the welcoming party?" she asked. "They're longing to meet you."

"Oh, yes, please," Robbie said, wriggling to get down.

"We're right behind you." Cal set his son down, watching him catch hold of Meredith's hand with the utmost trust and confidence. He was an amazingly friendly little fellow, remarkably self-possessed for his age. It was easy to see from his general behaviour and his advanced social skills Gina had raised him with a tender, loving hand. He also spoke very well and gave every appearance of being highly intelligent. He was a little son to be proud of.

A group of children had materialised—they had been kept in the shade of the hangar—making Robbie even more excited. They were the children of Coronation's staff, educated until the age of the ten at the small one-teacher schoolhouse on the station. All in all, it took some twenty emotion-packed minutes before the welcoming party broke up with another round of cheers led by the station's overseer, a very dashing young man called Steve Lockhart, before Cal was able to drive them to the homestead.

"That was the greatest thing ever!" Robbie exclaimed with satisfaction. "Everybody likes me."

"And why wouldn't they?" Meredith laughed, looking over Robbie's glossy head into his mother's eyes. "You're a great little boy!"

Time enough to see if Cal's parents like me, was Gina's thought. It didn't strike her as odd that Cal's parents hadn't come down to the airstrip to greet them. She supposed they might be people like the aunt Lorinda she well remembered. Cal had carried off the introductions with marvellous aplomb. No one looking at them both would have suspected things weren't as they seemed. As they had walked down the receiving line he had kept an arm lightly at her back, an expression of pride in her etched on his dynamic face. Steve Lockhart she recalled, had been observing them closely behind the charming welcoming smile. There was some strong connection between Meredith and Steve. She felt it keenly. But she also felt as far as the senior McKendricks were concerned staff would be expected to keep their distance. How then would that affect any friendship between Meredith and the station's impressive overseer? Gina recognised the quality in him.

They were received in the library. Good heavens, what a room! Gina thought. She could have fitted her entire apartment into the huge space. And *received* was the only way to put it. Cal's mother, a beautiful, well-preserved woman, dressed as though she were going to an important luncheon minus her hat and bag—glorious pearls—was seated in a wing chair. Cal's father, a very handsome man with piercing blue eyes was standing behind her. Another man, also standing, a few feet away, and bearing a close resemblance to Cal's father had to be Uncle Edward. Uncle Edward for a mercy looked kind and approachable. He was smiling, a lovely warm smile. Gina returned it with gratitude. This was certainly one good-looking family! But that was okay! The Romanos hadn't been behind the door when good looks were handed out. Rosa, too, was immensely attractive. Uncle Edward certainly appeared to think so going on his expression as his eyes came to rest on her.

Rosa, for her part, wasn't worried about the McKendricks. She could take them in her stride. What she was worried about, was how they would respond to her goddaughter. Looking after Gina was the reason Rosa was here.

Cal took the direct approach, making introductions. His

mother remained seated. They were all obliged to go to her. Gina could feel the little waves of resistance that emanated from the seated figure though Jocelyn spoke the right words as though she had learned them from a script. *Obviously she believes I've brought disruption and disgrace to the family,* Gina thought, shaking Jocelyn's unenthusiastic hand. There was no question of a hug much less a kiss. The handshake was as much as Gina could expect to get.

Cal's father, Ewan, after an initial moment of what appeared to be shock was quite genial by comparison. Gina caught him giving his wife a sharp, rebuking glance. She must have got the message because the charged atmosphere lightened somewhat. Friendly and outgoing as Robbie was, he had been half hiding behind his mother. Now Cal picked him up in his arms.

"This is your grandmother and grandfather, Robert. And that gentleman over there is my uncle Ed, your great-uncle. Say hello."

"Hello, everybody," Robbie piped up sweetly, looking around them all. Even at three he could recognise family going on appearance alone.

There were two spots of colour high up on Jocelyn's cheeks. Her green eyes that had appeared unfocused suddenly rested with great clarity on the little boy. "What a beautiful child you are!" she now exclaimed. "Come give Grandma a kiss." She held out her hand.

"Why he's the living image of you, Cal!" Ewan McKendrick burst out in triumph, his eyes settling with approval on the beautiful, self-composed young woman his son had brought home with him. This Gina, who he and Jocelyn had worried had no background at all, looked magnificent! He was quite taken aback. But what a blessing! "I want you to know, Gina, you're most welcome to the family. Most welcome."

Gina made no answer, but graciously inclined her head, unaware how very regal it appeared.

"And how good of you to accompany her, *signora*." Ewan's blue glance swept on to Gina's decidedly attractive companion. She was a damned sexy-looking woman. "May I call you Rosa?"

"But of course!" Rosa replied graciously.

"What, not going to shake hands with your grandfather, young man?" Ewan asked the little boy jovially, absolutely thrilled the boy was so clearly a McKendrick. What a plus!

Robbie went to him immediately. "I'm happy to meet you, Granddad."

Jocelyn chose that precise moment to burst into tears motivating Ed to jump into the void. "You must all want to rest after such a long flight?" he suggested, his eyes alighting more or less compulsively now on Rosa. She positively radiated life and vitality! Things couldn't get any better.

"Long but very smooth," Rosa assured him, meeting his gaze straight-on. There was a natural voluptuousness running like a ribbon through the accent Rosa had never lost. Now she took to studying with equal interest this tall, gentlemanly man with the blue, blue eyes and chivalrous expression. A widower she had been told. There was a strong attraction already between them. Could there be a little love for her around the corner? It was astonishing when and where love turned up.

Meredith who had been busy watching proceedings, spoke up. "One of the men will have taken your luggage to your rooms. I'll come up with you…help you settle in." It would give her mother time to compose herself, she thought.

"That will be lovely." Gina bestowed on her a grateful smile.

"You're coming, too, Daddy?" Robbie asked, looking back to his father with a melting smile.

"You bet I am," Cal assured him, though he remained where he was, a bracing hand on his mother's shoulder. "I'll be with you in a minute."

"Didn't you promise me you were going to teach me to ride a horse?" Robbie asked as though they might start the lessons now.

"A *pony,* Robert. I'll get one in especially for you."

"Oh, bravo!" Ewan McKendrick cried heartily. "It's only natural you have the love of horses in your blood, Robbie." My word, this was turning out well, Ewan thought. Jocelyn would just have to pull herself into line.

"Make this work, Mum." Cal bent to murmur in his mother's ear.

"Who said I haven't?" she replied haughtily, when the party were out of earshot. "At least she's beautiful." Even as she acknowledged the fact, Jocelyn felt a fierce stab of jealousy. She had always been Number One in her son's life. She had expected to remain Number One even if he had married the amenable Kym. This Gina was something else again. It wasn't easy to be supplanted. "As for the other one!" She threw up her hands.

Now it was Ed's turn to stun them. "Spellbinding, wasn't she? I just might ask her to marry me."

His handsome face wore a wide grin.

"You're joking of course!" Jocelyn looked at her brother-in-law with extreme disfavour.

Wasn't he?

Jocelyn, who had hardly eaten anything at dinner said good-night early and withdrew. Ewan, who couldn't completely disguise his anger with his wife, made his departure some time after.

Count on it. There would be words upstairs, Cal thought, angry and disappointed with his mother. He had never seen her so stiff and ungracious, even if he recognised her nose was out of joint. Both Gina and Rosa had that ineffable thing—glamour.

"You can stand in for me, Cal, at the party," Ewan said over his shoulder. "All they want is to see more of *you,* and Gina, not me!"

An overtired, overexcited Robbie had long since been tucked up in bed.

Rosa and Ed who had hit it off extremely well over dinner, the attraction continuing apace, had talked art among other things, Ed all the while staring at her in admiration. Now they expressed the desire to go along with the young ones to join the bar-b-que, which was in full swing judging by the sound of country-and-western music filling the air. Rosa who had wisely taken a short nap to look her best, showed no sign whatever of fatigue. Meredith, looking really beautiful, was also eager to join the party.

Cal detained Gina as the others moved off, chatting happily like old friends. "Let's go out on the terrace," he suggested. He needed privacy as two members of staff continued to hover in the dining room, checking that everything would be left just so.

"As you wish." Gina let him take her arm, unable to control her body's response to his touch. It made her feel extraordinarily vulnerable.

"Well, we lived through that," he offered dryly when they were out in the gardenia-scented night air. Inwardly, he was wondering if his father was going to throttle his mother.

"Your father is trying," Gina answered. "And Meredith and your uncle Ed are so kind, but it's just as I expected. Your mother doesn't and never will, like me."

My mother is jealous, Cal thought but couldn't bring himself to say it. "My mother is used to being in total control of the situation," he said by way of explanation. "This time she isn't. Don't let her bother you too much, Gina. She'll come around."

"If only for Robbie's sake." Gina took a calming breath. Inside love and hate were battling for her soul. "It's as well he looks like you. He'd have had no chance had he looked like me."

Cal glanced down at her, trying unsuccessfully to numb his own strong feelings. He had been watching her all night. She wore her hair the way he liked it. Loose, centre parted, flowing over her shoulders. Her dress was short and lacy, gold in colour. The low neckline showed her beautiful bosom to advantage, the skirt-length revealed her long sexy legs. "It so happens I'm praying for a daughter who looks just like you."

"You may have a long wait," she said coolly.

"Then I'll just have to seduce you all over again. That's what you think I did, isn't it? Seduce you? Because, you know, I thought the attraction was mutual?"

"I don't remember." She turned her face away.

"Liar." He led her down the short flight of stone steps. "Ed seems to have taken quite a shine to Rosa?" There was amusement and surprise in his voice.

"Sometimes you just never know what people are capable of," Gina said. "Your uncle has been alone a long time?"

"Ten years. His wife, Aunt Jenny, was a lovely person. I remember Meredith crying her heart out at the funeral. I wanted to, but couldn't. Men don't cry and all that. I had to bite my lip until I drew blood."

"So you do have a heart after all?"

It wasn't a tease. She sounded serious. "Oh ,well, while we're at it, where have you stowed yours?"

She tossed back a long sable lock. "I have Robbie. My son is everything in life to me. That's the only way you got me here, Cal. You gave me no option but—"

"To stage a battle you'd very likely lose," he finished for her. "Now, what about if we call a truce while we're on show. Remember, we're supposed to be lovers, cruelly separated for so long now to be gloriously reunited in marriage."

She laughed though her heart was beating like a drum. "Don't think I'm taking off on any honeymoon," she warned. "And don't think we're going to finish up in the same bed."

"*Gianina, mia,* it's not as though I've actually asked you to have sex," he mocked. "But never fear. I will get around to it." His voice grew more serious. "I thought we might defer the honeymoon until Robert is more used to the family. Or we could take him with us?"

She stopped moving, visibly agitated. "Where on earth are you thinking?"

"Need you ask, the island?" Now, what was the matter with him, baiting her like that, because she reacted like that was the cruellest thing he could have said.

"You must be mad."

He shrugged. "That's the sad thing. You *made* me mad. Good and mad. Tell me what happened on the island, Gina. You can make it brief if it pains you to speak."

She glanced up at the twinkling fairy lights strung through the trees. Their glow swept the grass and illuminated the garden beds that were filled with rich tropical flowers, the fragrance intoxicating in the warm air. "What are you trying to trap me into saying? I told you I don't want to discuss the past. Suffice to say I fell in love unwisely but too well."

"You jumped right in."

"So did you."

"I shared your reckless streak," he freely admitted. "You were my Juliet. The girl I thought I could die for."

"No tragedy, a farce."

"We have Robert, don't we?" he said in a low voice.

"Yes," she answered quietly.

"I should tell you I intend to have a long talk with my aunt when she gets back home. I have an idea she had more to do with events than I'd realised."

"The past is ancient history. I'm determined to move forwards.

So where is your aunt? Does she take off on her broom stick now and again?"

It was said with such scorn, he stopped in his tracks. "Where did that come from all of a sudden?"

Immediately she made a rueful face. "That was a slip. I withdraw it." She had to close a door on the past now that this new door had opened. His aunt would always remain family. She would always be around. "I would never go back to the island," she said, changing the subject. "It was another time."

"I wouldn't go back, either," he said crisply.

"You were just being cruel then?"

"I feel cruel towards you once in a while."

She felt her heart contract. "Small wonder I'm scared of you."

"I should think you would be," he replied, glancing down at her.

They walked on through the tropical night, the path overshadowed by magnificent broad-domed shade trees. "I don't want any big wedding, Cal," she said nervously.

"So why don't you make a list of a few close friends?" he suggested in a suave tone. "I don't want any big wedding, either."

"I have no intention of dressing like a bride, either."

"What?" He brought them to a halt. "When you'll make a *glorious* bride?"

She bit her lip, her body aching at his closeness, her mind bent on running away. "I'm the mother of a three-year-old boy."

"High time you got married then," he commented. "I have to insist you dress the part. I'm not going to be denied my trophy wife. That's part of the deal."

They moved on. "Would you like me to ask your Kym to be a bridesmaid?" she asked silkily.

"You'd have to be really crazy to do that."

"Stranger things have happened. I know someone who invited all his old girlfriends to his wedding."

"You were one of them?"

"Never! I'm a one-man woman at heart." Damn why had she said that?

"I'll disregard that. The only man you'll ever be allowed to get romantic over is *me*."

"That's not going to be a lot of fun."

"Why are you working so hard to hate me?"

She gave a brittle laugh. "That's a lot of question, Cal. Loving you turned out to be very, very painful."

"Surely you made me pay keeping Robert from me." His hurt, his sorrow, his impotent rage burst through his lips.

Gina reacted fiercely. So fiercely Cal was forced to pull her to him, silencing any tempestuous outburst of hers by covering her mouth with his own. "People can see us," he muttered, against her gritted teeth.

How very stupid of her! An anguished moan escaped her throat. People, of course. She had to keep her wits about her, yet every time she was alone with him she thought them sealed off from the rest of the world. Ever so slowly she managed to pull herself together. Even that wildly discordant kiss had made her knees buckle.

"You shouldn't say things like that to me," she censured him, shaking back the silky hair that was spilling around her hot face.

"I'll let you go when you say sorry."

She could hear the taunt in his voice. "You'll let me go *now*. I'm just mad enough to scream. Besides, I can't run away."

"That's right," he agreed. "You can't. You look beautiful. Did I tell you? I love that dress."

"I thought you might like it," she said, tartly.

"Oh, I do. It shows off your beautiful figure. Your mouth tastes of peaches and champagne."

"I've had both," she pointed out. "Shall we walk on?"

"Why not?" he agreed suavely. "Arm in arm like a happily married couple."

"And just how long do you think this marriage will last?"

"Well, let's see now. It's the start of the twenty-first century," he said musingly. "Hopefully we'll have a good fifty years, probably more. The thing is, when you said yes to marrying me, Gina, in my book that means *for ever.*"

The expression on his handsome face looked a lot more like ruthless than loving.

Steven had reached the stage where he thought she wasn't going to make an appearance that night. The evening was a great success. No effort had been spared to ensure Coronation's staff would find it memorable. The food was great—as always—Coronation's premier beef, numerous side dishes, hot and cold, salads galore. Icy-cold beer was on tap to stimulate the appetite, soft drinks and fruit juices for the children—they were still running around—wine for the ladies. The dessert table—a mecca for anyone with a sweet tooth—was a long trestle covered with a white linen cloth. It was laden with dishes that looked like they had been prepared by a master chef dedicated to that sort of thing. He circulated constantly—it was part of his job—still, she didn't come.

Then he saw her.

His mood lifted to the skies. She was walking with Gina's aunt Rosa and Edward McKendrick. He really liked Ed, who was vastly more approachable than his elder brother. Gina's aunt, he realised, was an unconventional dresser but he thought she looked great in her vividly coloured outfit. It was sort of gypsy-ish, embroidered with something glinting. From the body language Ed seemed to think she looked fantastic. Good for you, Ed, Steven thought. It was a tragedy what had happened to Ed's wife—a lovely woman from all accounts—but eventually one had to get on with life.

Meredith stopped his breath. She wore a dress, a beautiful deep blue dress. He had seldom seen her in a dress, not even at the polo matches or informal functions Coronation hosted from time to time. She mostly wore jeans or tailored pants. Why not? Hers was the ideal figure to show them off. But tonight she wore something filmy and to him desperately romantic. Romance his soul craved. Did women realise men were every bit as romantic as they were? The fabric of her floaty skirt wrapped itself around her lithe body as she moved. Her wonderful hair was loose, falling in a shiny waterfall down her back.

Ed came towards him, extending his hand. "Everything going well, Steve?"

"Everyone's having a great time, Mr McKendrick." Steve returned the smile and the handshake, shifting his gaze to Meredith and Aunt Rosa. "Good evening, ladies. May I say how beautiful you both look?"

"Certainly you may!" Rosa nodded her dark head, her thick hair short and expertly cut. "I think there is something a little bit dangerous about you, Steven." She waved a finger.

"No worries." Steve smiled back at her. "It's just that I like women. Are Cal and Gina coming?" He glanced towards the main path.

"Right behind us," Meredith said, surprising herself greatly by going to him and taking his arm. Never once had she done that. "I think I'd like a cold drink. What about you?" Her gaze moved from Rosa to her uncle, who overnight looked ten years younger with a renewed zest for life.

"You two go on ahead," Ed answered in a relaxed voice, "Rosa and I will stroll for a bit."

Rosa took Ed's arm companionably. "You must tell me everything I need to know about your magnificent gardens, Edward."

Her intriguing accent made not two but three sensuous syllables of *Ed-ah-ward*. "I'm longing to explore them by daylight."

"And I'd be delighted to show you," Ed responded gallantly. "That wonderfully exotic fragrance on the air is from the many, many beds of yellow-throated Asian lilies, the pinks, the whites and the creams."

"Why, yes, I can see them glowing in the dark," Rosa said. "I would love to paint them."

"Then you must have your chance."

"Why is it I think Ed has taken a great liking to Gina's aunt Rosa?" Steve asked as Ed and Rosa moved away across the grass.

"She's an extremely attractive woman and a woman of culture." Meredith smiled. "She and Ed got into a discussion on art at the dinner table. Both of them are well informed, but I could see Dad was rather bored. He and Ed look very much alike but their personalities are completely different."

"How did the little dinner party go?" Steve asked. "Are your parents going to make an appearance tonight?"

Meredith shook her head, mightily relieved. "Mum retired early. Dad followed. I expect they might have a few words when they're alone. Mum scarcely pretended a veneer of charm over dinner."

"That's awful." Steve winced. "I would have thought your parents would be delighted to have such a beautiful woman for a daughter-in-law. And Robbie is a great little kid, full of life and so well spoken for his age. Mother and son made a really good impression with the staff. So did Rosa. Everyone on the station is full of praise for them and delight for Cal. That's why the evening is going so wonderfully well. Everyone's happy."

"Are *you* happy, Steven?" She stared up at him, the bronze of his skin in striking contrast to the snowy white shirt he wore with his tight fitting jeans. For herself, she was glowing inside, certain now she was in love.

"I am now you're here," he said softly, gazing down at her. "I was beginning to get worried you mightn't make an appearance."

"Nothing would have kept me away." She gripped his arm tighter, a gesture Steve found utterly enchanting. It was all he could do not to turn her into his arms. Alas, there were too many people around. "I meant it when I said you look beautiful. You dazzle me. You're a *dream* in a dress, especially one that floats all around you."

"Why thank you, Steven." She smiled, stars in her eyes.

He bent his head to her urgently. "I want to kiss you."

"I want to kiss you back."

Only voices intervened. *"Hi, Steve! Good evening, Ms McKendrick!"*

"Hello there!" Meredith responded brightly, lifting her hand to return the greetings.

"Can't we go somewhere *quiet?*" Even as he said it Steve couldn't help laughing. They would have to get right out of the home compound to find silence. Someone had turned the music up louder. Someone else toned it down a little. People were dancing.

"Not tonight I'm afraid." She sighed with deep regret. "Cal and Gina will be along soon. Why don't we join in the dancing?"

"Do you think that's wise?"

"It's too late to talk about being wise now, Steven," she said, yearning to be in his arms.

Steven came back to himself for a minute. "I don't want to put you into any stressful situation. Your happiness is very important to me, Meredith."

"So you're *not* going to dance with me?" She tilted her head to one side.

"Are you asking me if I'm game?" he responded to the challenge.

"Something like that, Steven Lockhart."

His smile faltered slightly. "But I'm not a Lockhart, am I? I'm not a Lancaster, either. What *am* I to you, Meredith?"

She reached up to gently touch his mouth, tracing the outline of his lower lip, beautifully cut and undeniably sensual. "You're too touchy."

"I want to touch *you*," he said, his voice mesmerizing. "I want to very gently unwrap you from your beautiful clothes. You can't be wearing a bra, not in that dress?" His golden-brown eyes moved over the tiny bodice with its thin straps, cut to reveal her décolletage.

"There's one built into the dress," she explained, aware her voice shook. It felt like he was stroking her. Featherlike strokes that ranged over her throat and down to the upward curves of her breasts.

The music had changed to a ballad.

He took her into his arms. Wasn't this what he had been longing for all night?

Other couples were dancing beneath the trees, some were twirling down the paths. Some were just having fun. Others were intent on each other.

He was a beautiful mover. She knew that from the way he walked.

They were perfectly quiet. There was no need for words. The intense communication came from the sizzling proximity of their bodies. She was falling fathoms deep into a bottomless lagoon of sexual hunger. It surpassed anything she had felt before. She had to go further, much further than kisses. She let him steer her this way and that, her heart beating madly. If only they didn't have to stop. She wasn't even sure she *could* stop.

"Meredith!" Somewhere a little distance off, amid the babble of laughter and music, her father's voice cracked out.

"God, it's your dad," Steve muttered, "and he's heading this way."

He didn't release her, however. He made no move to. "I

thought he was supposed to have retired for the night?" he asked, the merest thread of humour in a dead calm voice.

"I thought he had."

Still, he held her.

"Good evening, Mr McKendrick," Steve greeted his boss smoothly. "We weren't certain if we were going to have the pleasure of your company this evening."

Ewan McKendrick stopped right in front of them. "So you took advantage of the situation by thinking you could dance with my daughter?" he retorted in an insufferably arrogant tone.

Steve kept a tight rein on his temper and his tone low. People were starting to look their way, aware things weren't quite right. "Excuse me, sir, is there a law against that?" There was no trace of insolence in his voice, just a simple question requiring a simple answer.

Meredith's nerves were fluttering badly. "Please, Dad! You're drawing attention to us."

Her father ignored her. Fresh from a humdinger of an argument with his wife, he was ready for blood. "Would you mind letting my daughter go?" he said thickly, reaching out to shove Steve away, but Steve, a good thirty years younger and superbly fit, didn't budge. He did, however, drop his hands not wanting to further inflame an already inflammable situation.

Some distance away Gina felt that warning finger on her nape. She began to walk faster.

"It's good you're so eager to join the party." Cal laughed, stepping it out with her.

"Something is wrong up ahead," she told him, sounding serious. "I feel you should be there."

Cal didn't ask her what she meant. He had seen in Gina a lot of things beyond her physical beauty.

It was as she said. Cal saw with dismay his father give Steve Lockhart a hard shove in the shoulder. It had no effect so far as he could see on Steve, but it told him all he needed to know. A head-to-head confrontation was already in place. Meredith's body language spoke of embarrassment and anguish. Poor Merri! She looked so beautiful tonight. She didn't have to take this sort of thing. Their father was as dictatorial a man as he had ever met, whereas Steve had earned his trust and deserved respect.

"Your parents would do well to step into the twenty-first century," Gina murmured, shaking her head. It was inevitable she would be on Steve's side.

"I can't help but agree," Cal gritted, increasing his pace. "They run Coronation Hill like their own kingdom." It wasn't something he was proud of. He glanced down at Gina, not wanting to draw her into it. "You might like to stay here."

She shook her head. "I'll come with you."

"It might get sticky."

"I have no doubt you can handle it."

They closed in on the trio fast. "Hey, everything okay here?" he called, the heavy tension in the atmosphere coming at them in a wave.

Ewan McKendrick rounded on his son. "You *can't* be talking to *me!*"

"Actually, yes, Dad," Cal said, coolly quiet.

Out of the corner of her eye Gina saw people moving quickly away from what looked like shaping up to be a war zone. Most of the staff would have taken note of the fact their very popular overseer was dancing with the boss's daughter. Not only that, but *how* they were dancing. Hadn't she divined an involvement between Meredith and Steve Lockhart, within the first few minutes?

"You're upset, Dad," Cal spoke to his father soothingly, knowing words had most likely passed between his parents. "Why don't I accompany you back to the house?"

"What am I supposed to make of this?" Ewan demanded of his son. "I come out for a breath of air and to make an appearance and what should I be confronted by but my daughter snuggling up to this fella here." He stabbed a condemnatory finger in Steve's direction. "Didn't you see what was going on?"

"Dancing, Dad. All quite respectable," Cal answered reasonably. "You've overreacted. Merri can dance with whomever she pleases."

"Not while she's under *my* roof," Ewan returned furiously.

"Your roof, certainly," Cal agreed. "My roof, Mum's roof, Merri's roof, Ed's roof."

"No need whatever to include me!" Gina broke in ironically, vividly reminded of how her own father had tyrannized her male friends.

"Gina, darling," Cal stressed, "You and Robbie go with *me*." He returned his attention to his father. "Let's go, Dad. Don't spoil what has been a pleasant evening. I think you owe Steve an apology. He's done no wrong."

Ewan's handsome face reddened. "He hasn't, eh? I gave you more credit, Calvin. Lockhart here has a larger purpose than being our overseer. Mark my words. He has designs on my daughter, *your* sister, I might remind you."

"You're absolutely right, sir," Steve broke in, "I do think the world of Meredith."

"Indeed!" Ewan thundered, now totally enraged. "You just keep away from her, fella. I have in mind someone from a fine family for my only daughter. Not a no-one like you!"

They were all startled by his tone, swept with vehemence.

"That's it, Dad!" Cal got a firm grip on his father before Steve lost it. He was about to, judging from his expression. "It would help a lot if you come away."

Ewan McKendrick shook his head several times as if to clear it. "The fella's a bastard!" he ground out heavily. "No way could you ever be good enough for my daughter. You're fired, Lockhart. Don't try to go against me, Cal. I'm still in charge of Coronation and don't you forget it."

"I'm not forgetting it, Dad," Cal said very quietly, yet his voice carried an effortless authority. "But I'm relying on you to regain your common sense. Steve is very good at what he does. You can't expect me to carry the burden without him. Come along now. Your blood pressure was up the last time the doctor took a look at you."

"Why wouldn't it be up in this family?" Ewan McKendrick glowered, but he allowed himself to be led away.

Gina reacted first. She reached out a hand to the distressed Meredith, who clasped it tightly. "My father used to interfere in all my friendships, Meredith," she lamented. "I was never allowed to bring a boy home. Only girlfriends were allowed. As I got older no one was good enough for me. I was my father's 'shining star.' He always called me that. When I fell pregnant he literally threw me out."

Meredith and Steve were so shocked by that admission they momentarily forgot their own outraged feelings. "Gina, how dreadful!" Meredith was aghast. "I never thought—"

"I've never spoken about it," Gina said. "My mother gave me whatever money she had spirited away. Somehow I was able to finish my degree. I didn't show until the seventh month, which helped a lot. I didn't tell anyone. Only Rosa knew. I couldn't have done without Rosa. She's been an enormous support to me and wonderful to Robbie. You can't allow your father to run your life, Meredith. Please don't think *I* am now interfering in your personal affairs. I do so out of my own experience and concern for you."

"I know that, Gina." Meredith shook her head utterly dismayed. "Does Cal know this?"

Gina smiled sadly. "One day I'll tell him."

"You should tell him now."

Gina shook her head. "There are still a few issues we have to work through. I'll know the time."

"Of course you will." Meredith backed off. "How mortifying this all is. What must you think of us?"

Gina spoke directly. "Your mother doesn't like me, Meredith. I doubt she ever will. Your father will try. But I'm not sure I can live under the same roof as a mother-in-law who so clearly doesn't approve of me."

"What are you saying, Gina?" Meredith's voice rose in alarm.

"I'm saying if I'm not happy here I mightn't be able to stay." Gina's beautiful face took on an adamant cast. Gina had had more than her share of dysfunctional families.

"You've told Cal how you feel?" Steve asked. He was still fuming inside, having come very close to punching McKendrick in the nose. Cal had known it. That was why he had spirited his father away.

"No, but I will if it becomes necessary," Gina said, with a note of resolve in her voice. She knew if Meredith and Steve didn't, Cal wasn't about to let her leave. For *any* reason. By the same token she knew he wasn't going to allow his mother to continue on her present course. She looked back into two distressed faces, as much for her as themselves, she realised with gratitude. "I was surprised and very touched by my welcoming party when we arrived," she told them. "I'd like you to know that. I suppose it's normal enough for your mother, Meredith, to have difficulties accepting me. I'm not the daughter-in-law she wanted. Kym, wasn't it? Your aunt, Lorinda, told me all about her." In the stress of the moment that withheld piece of information spilled out.

"So it had to be when we were on the island?" Meredith's face darkened with a frown.

Immediately Gina made a little dismissive gesture with her hands. "Sorry. I've said too much already. Cal doesn't know. I'd prefer the past to stay in the past, Meredith. It will do no good to rake it all up. Now, if you'll excuse me, I'll carry out Cal's wishes and mingle with the staff for a while. I expect he'll be back soon."

Meredith looked at Steven in sharp dismay. She could see he shared her feelings. "Please remember Cal needs you desperately, Gina."

Gina didn't answer but turned away with an enigmatic little smile.

Cal needs his *son* desperately, Gina amended in her own mind.

Left alone, Meredith put a conciliatory hand on Steve's arm.

"Careful," he warned, his lean body taut.

"Please don't be like that, Steven," she begged. "I am so sorry, but it's not my fault.'

Or maybe it *is,* she thought wretchedly. She should have protected Steven. That meant leaving him well alone.

"It would have given me a great deal of pleasure to have punched your father in the nose," he said tightly.

"I think we all knew that, Steven. My father can be unbelievably arrogant. In some ways my parents don't know a lot about *real* life."

"They're too protected by their wealth," Steve diagnosed accurately. "But I suppose it's not all that surprising. Isn't God a McKendrick?"

His tone cut. "He *can't* fire you."

"He *can* fire me," Steve corrected, his attractive voice oddly harsh.

"Cal will speak to him. He'll listen."

"You think so?" Steve threw up his hands. "I think it more

likely you'll disappear overseas. Join your gadfly aunt who appears to have done some mischief whether Gina wants to keep her out of it or not. As for you, you'll come home and marry your father's nominee. None of your family will accept me, Meredith, outside of Cal and Gina. And that would only make it hard for them both."

Anger came, swift and unexpected. "Shouldn't you be worrying more about whether *I'll* accept you?" she cried.

That settled it for Steve. "I'll be out of here by midday tomorrow, okay?" he said curtly. "Maybe sooner. It's been great knowing you, Meredith. Tell Gina if she wants a normal life then she sure picked the wrong family."

She ran after him, mortified. "Steven, please don't go." She made an effort to catch his shirt, and almost lost her footing on the exposed root of a tree.

He didn't notice and kept going, taking swift, powerful strides away from her.

Meredith gave up. Her father had made sure of it calling Steven a bastard. How dare he?

See what you've gone and done? the voice in her head taunted. *You should have left him alone. You knew what was going to happen. You fool you! Getting to think things might be different. Nothing will ever change around here. Not until it's Cal's turn to reign.*

Steven, she knew, had been sitting pretty as Coronation's overseer, a position of trust and responsibility. He had security and earned good money. It would be highly unlikely he could find a comparable position in the near future. She wasn't even sure if Cal could persuade her father to relent even if Steven agreed to stay. And that didn't look like it was happening. Not from the way he had stormed off.

Meredith returned to the house feeling sick to her soul.

CHAPTER SIX

READY for bed, Gina looked in on Robbie, whose bedroom was just across the hallway from hers. She opened the door very quietly, widening the opening so a golden ray of light fell across his face. She had left a small night-light burning in any case. It was possible he could awake some time during the night and feel disorientated in a strange house. She didn't really expect him to. It was Robbie's practice to fall asleep as soon as his head hit the pillow, sleeping right through until she woke him by pulling the lobe of his ear very gently in the morning. It was a trick that always worked.

Just as she thought, he was fast asleep, clutching his favourite teddy bear. Her face softened into an expression of the utmost maternal tenderness. Robbie wouldn't go anywhere without that bear. His father had promised him the room would be redecorated in any way he liked. Maybe a few lighter touches here and there, but it was a beautiful big airy room with French doors leading out onto a broad verandah. It was a full moon outside; the big copper moon of the tropics. She had to say it affected her.

She wanted Cal. She wanted him to come to her. She wanted to hear his voice.

How could you love a man so passionately when he had broken your heart?

Gently, she closed Robbie's door. His room had a different view from hers, overlooking the extensive gardens that led to the large stables complex at the rear of the house. Coronation Hill's homestead was very impressive, she thought. A huge substantial house, it had evolved, so Cal had told her, from the original single-storey stone colonial cottage. One would never have known it. Today it was a lofty two-storey structure with the central section linking two long wings. Obviously the generations of McKendricks had spared no expense developing a homestead that befitted their station.

She returned to her own room, feeling bruised, emotionally and spiritually. How could this possibly work out? Even Meredith's developing relationship with the extremely attractive Steven Lockhart seemed heading for a shipwreck.

"Damn!" she said out loud, giving one of the pillows several good thumps.

"Bad as that, is it?"

She looked up to see Cal standing in the open doorway. His handsome face wore a brooding expression. It was obvious he, too, was deeply disturbed.

"Need you ask?" Another minute and she would have shut her door. Would he have knocked?

He sighed in a way that told her the events of the evening had well and truly taken their toll. "May I come in?"

She shrugged. "Shut the door after you. Robbie's asleep. So tell me what's happening about Steve? Did you manage to persuade your father to change his mind about sacking him?"

"I can handle my father," said Cal, thrusting a hand through his thick mahogany hair. "It's Steve I'm worried about. Meredith has come back to the house in a hell of a state. Sometimes I think there's not a guy in the world who would pass first base with Dad."

"Meredith can't live her whole life being dictated to."

Cal shrugged. "Of course she can't. But I don't think there's been anyone who really mattered to her up to this date. No one to really push for. Steve would seem to be different. She said he told her he was leaving in the morning."

"Oh, no!" Gina looked back at him in dismay. "Have you spoken to him?"

"I'm giving him some space. Hoping he'll cool off. He can't get anywhere until the freight plane gets in around noon."

"And Meredith?"

"What about her?" His jewel-like eyes moved over her, studying her hungrily. The muscles of his thighs tensed as his body stirred. No make-up, long hair tied back at the nape, a shell-pink satin robe sashed tightly at the waist, slippers on her feet. She still looked glorious, he thought with a hot burn of desire that was exposed in his eyes.

"Is she going to give in without a fight?" Gina's breathing started to come rather fast. Labour as she might, she still couldn't keep her physical yearning for him under control. Just to look at him triggered a response.

"*We* did, didn't we?" He suddenly flung himself down on the end of her huge four poster bed, falling backwards with a groan.

Ohhh! Gina didn't feel she was any way near strong enough for such temptations. "Why was your father so horrible to Steve?" Autocrat or not Ewan McKendrick's reaction had seemed excessive.

"Because Dad can be bloody horrible sometimes." Cal addressed the ornately plastered ceiling. "For a man like my father, a family liaison with a staff member is *verboten.*"

Gina moved well away from the bed. Hadn't her liaison with him been forbidden? "*Mein Gott,* German!" she said with a flash of sarcasm. "And the bastard bit? That was appalling. I was shocked."

Cal remained lying where he was, as though it would cost him too much of a physical effort to get up. "Steve is the natural son of one of our biggest beef producers," he explained. "A man called Gavin Lancaster. Lancaster took a fancy to Steve's mother many long years ago and Steve is the result. He's so much a Lancaster everyone in the Outback knows."

"And Lancaster knows presumably?"

"Of course."

"But he chooses not to recognise his own son?" There was a throb of outrage in her voice.

"I'm very sorry to say the answer's yes."

Gina felt a great rush of pity for Steve Lockhart. "This Lancaster can't be a man of character and heart. That's terrible, Cal. And Steve's mother?"

"She was married at the time. Somehow managed to patch the marriage up. The family—he has two half brothers and a half sister—moved to New Zealand when Steve was fourteen. He's been on his own since. Surprisingly, however, they did put him in a very good boarding school before they left."

"Oh, that was nice of them!" Gina scoffed.

"Wasn't it? He was with other boys from landed families. That's how he remained on the land. Love for the land is something that runs deep in the blood. Steve has it."

"Poor Steve!" Gina looked towards the moonlit verandah and beyond that the night under stars. "The bar-b-que must have folded. The music has stopped."

"I think Dad's performance put paid to the evening," Cal groaned. "But they got a good few hours in."

"Steve's in love with Meredith," Gina said, a poignant expression on her beautiful face.

"He may well be but he's a proud man. Come here a moment." He raised his dark head slightly off the bed.

"You can't stay." She didn't move.

"Shall I get out now?" he asked, and gave a low laugh.

"No, you don't have to go *right* now."

"Many thanks, *principessa!*" he mocked. "Bear with me for a little while. That's all I ask."

All? She was near mad for him to touch her. Their sexual attraction was so strong she did right to fear it. Excitement was growing at a great pace inside her. She tried, but failed to keep it down. He knew exactly how to press her every last button. To move nearer the bed, would be akin to going in at the deep end.

When she was little more than a tentative foot away, he suddenly made a grab for her. "Gotcha!" He pulled her to him with a fierceness that still held an element of cherishing.

They were both on the bed in one swift motion, he half on top of her, running his hand down her shoulder to her waist to the top of her long slender leg, stopping while he looked deep into her eyes.

"I finally get you home and it's all bad news. Well, not entirely. Robbie has the magic key to everyone's heart. I'm sorry for the way my mother behaved at dinner. I apologise for her. I get mad just thinking about it, but it wasn't the time to bring on a big family argument. That might have to wait, but you can bet your life she got an earful from Dad."

Gina felt like she was about to cry but decided she could not. He lowered his face into her neck, his mouth moving against her skin. "Oh, you smell *wonderful!* Like a million wildflowers!"

She could feel the weight of his head on her shoulder. He had his eyes closed, just lying there breathing her in. "Things have got to change, Gina," he muttered against her skin. "Just hang in there. I'm going to make them change. I know how." *I can't lose her,* Cal thought. *Not all over again.*

The ache of tears was in Gina's throat. She couldn't help herself. She placed her palm very tenderly against his cheek. When she surrendered, she surrendered. It was part of her nature. What was the point of all this alternating between love and hate? They were tied to one another, weren't they? They shared their son.

"Gina?" He opened his eyes to stare at her. She had never seen eyes like his before she had met him. That amazing jewel-like green. Now she had a child with those same eyes.

Cal lifted his torso supporting his body with his strong arms. "Would you let me love you?"

Heat grew to flame. She knew he would be true to his word, giving her the opportunity to say yes, or decline his advances. If she said no would she always look back at this moment and regret it? Or should she open herself up to him? She had kept maintaining the past was best forgotten. She even acted on it, in not implicating his aunt in her banishment from the island. Shouldn't she look to the future? Shouldn't she take the first step?

As if to goad her the voice inside her head said: *Because you want it...want it...want it!* Sexual needs had their own sovereignty. Her need for him was urgent.

Cal saw the change come over her. He saw the powerful feelings that drove her. Feelings that left little place for pride or any other consideration. Nothing could stand up against the raw passion they had for each other.

Gina's hand came up compulsively and found the buttons of his shirt. She slid them free from their buttonholes. She could smell the special male fragrance of his skin, as intoxicating to her as her fragrance was to him. She could feel his warmth, the texture of the whorls of dark hair on his chest, spearing through it with her fingers while his whole body tensed. She must have been taking too long because abruptly he helped her, stripping his shirt roughly from him and flinging it away.

His shadow fell over her. He held her hands away as he bent to kiss her open mouth, pouring such passion into and over her she was drenched. Then he was removing her clothes, folding his face into them, and when she was naked his hands began to move over her commanding her body to obey. It was a primitive kind of mastery; dominant male over female, but it was made all the more fantastic because it seemed to Gina to be overlaid with a ravishing tenderness. He wasn't so much intent on his own pleasure. He was intent on *hers*.

"Tell me you can find it within yourself to love me?" His hands enclosed the golden globes of her breasts, the darkening rose-coloured nipples swollen and erect.

"I *did* love you." Her eyes were closed to him, as though open they would reveal too much of herself to him.

"Or so you said." His hand began to trace a line from her navel down to the quivering apex of her body with its delicate cleft. He dipped his head and kissed her there.

Sensations shot through her as keen as a blade.

She shuddered, her voice barely audible. "I believed all *you* said to me then." Her back began to arch and flex. The impact of his mouth on her sex was enormous.

"But you can't believe me now?" He took his time over his ministrations, all the while watching her face, a clear barometer for the raging emotions he was arousing in her.

"All I want is for our son…to…be happy." She could only gasp out the words, her body was in such a throbbing state of arousal.

"*I* don't matter?" Now his fingers found their way inside her.

"Of course you matter," she gasped, her back arching off the bed as he explored deeper. "I can't talk. I can't *talk*." Sensation was eclipsing everything else, requiring her most intense concentration.

"You're going to marry me."

His voice sounded deep in her ear.

"Yes!" she moaned hoarsely.

He levered himself over her, a lean powerful man yet she

couldn't seem to feel his weight. She *adored* his body on top of hers. Worshipped it. Now her own hand began to move, certain of what he wanted. She heard with a certain triumph, the harsh catch of his breath.

"Gina!" He groaned as if he were in the most exquisitely excruciating pain.

"I'm here!" She carried on tormenting him, until he could scarcely bear it. Then in a galvanic surge he reversed their positions. She was on top of him, her legs locked around him, muscles taut, her long hair tumbling forwards as she bent to kiss his marvellous mouth.

"Will this pass for love?" she softly taunted, armed with the knowledge in her lovemaking he found her faultless.

His voice was a near-satiated growl in his throat. "If it isn't, don't let it ever end."

From long habit Cal awoke in the predawn. The sky outside was a luminous pearl-grey, the horizon shot through with filmy layers of pink, gold and mauve. They were lying spooned together, front to back, her beautiful body curved into his, his arm lying over the top of her, the tips of his fingers resting on her breast. He felt his body instantly react, but first he just wanted to look at her sleeping face, to savour the miracle of her presence beside him. He no longer had just memories to live with. He had the woman. Whatever the difficulties of the past, the difficulties that lay ahead, this part of their relationship was perfect. He couldn't imagine lovemaking more ravishing. He swore he could hear the beat of her heart. Surely it matched his own?

She sighed deeply and began to turn, eyelids flickering, a frown shadowing her face, her lips murmuring, *"No!"*

His hand tightened over the satin slope of her shoulder. "Gina, you're dreaming." He shook her. "Gina?" There was real anguish in that moan.

A handful of seconds later and she opened her eyes, huge and velvety dark. "Cal!" She looked as if she were still lost in a wilderness of emotions.

"Are you okay? You were having a bad dream."

She shivered though the room was pleasantly warm. "I was back on the island."

"So why did it make you want to cry?"

She stared up into his eyes. "What *did* you really feel for me then, Cal, *what?* Please tell me."

He pushed her back gently into the pillows. He couldn't bear to tarnish the memory of what they had.

She closed her eyes against that telling expression on his face. "I'm sorry."

"You should be sorry." He bent and kissed her. A kiss that seemed to go on and on for ever. "I'm crazy about you," he muttered as he withdrew his mouth from hers. *"Crazed."*

This time when they made love it couldn't have been more different from the night before. This time their coming together was more a clash. It was almost as though each was still out for revenge. Unresolved revenge for four long years of pain and grief. Were they damned by all their complex issues? A man could be crazy about a woman without wanting it, without even loving her. Gina had believed herself abandoned at the most crucial turning point in her life. She had had to bring a child into the world without the love and support of its father; Cal felt himself betrayed by the girl, who in the shortest space of time, barely six weeks, had become everything in the world to him. The girl who had the power to destroy his ordered life. The girl who had denied him all knowledge of his son. There were, without question, powerful issues yet to be worked through.

But physically, they thrashed in the bed together, in an orgy of desire, playing out their past torments while their demons were let loose. Cal thrust into her powerfully, one hand behind her high arching back, her hoarse little cries serving only to drive him on.

When it was over they lay back utterly shaken by the primitive forces that had taken them over.

"Did I hurt you?" God, had he intended to, even for a moment? he castigated himself.

"No, though I seem to have left my mark on you." She could see her nail marks on his shoulders and on the small of his hard muscled back. "Let's take a shower," she suggested, aware her voice sounded as fragile as she felt. "That's when I can get my breath back."

"Here, let me help you." He rose from his side of the bed and came round to her, the splendid male, lifting her naked body high in his arms.

Under the warm silver stream of water, she let him cover her with a soft lather of sandalwood-scented soap: over her face, the long stem of her throat, down over her breasts, the smoothness of her stomach, between her legs, right down to her toes. She had thought herself satiated, yet she was trembling all over again, her stomach sucked in. She realised she couldn't get enough of him. Quite simply he filled her with passion in every pore of her skin. He was holding her strongly beneath the arms as the torrent of water washed over them; virtually holding her up. Her back was pressed up against the cold, slick tiles. He was moving into her body, moving rhythmically, driving slow and deep until he found her very core. The expression on his downbent dark face glistening with water was heart poundingly rapt.

Gina had the strangest sensation they were becoming one person. Then all thought was lost in a rush of violent desire.

* * *

Cal had been sitting outside the overseer's bungalow for maybe ten minutes before Steve drove up. He got out of the station ute, mopping the sweat from his face with the red bandana he had worn around his neck. He walked up the couple of steps with no sign of surprise.

"I've sent Mike and a couple of the boys to bring in the clean-skins at the ravine."

"Good." Cal nodded. "Have you decided what you're going to do?"

"I reckon your dad decided that," Steve said. "Look, would you like a cup of coffee?"

"I won't say no." Cal stood up, both men going inside the comfortable bungalow furnished in a simple palette of white with a turquoise-blue feature wall in the living area to offset the polished timber floor, the big Thai coffee table and the brown leather sofa and matching armchairs. The station had provided all the furnishings. Steve had added a few pleasing touches.

"Take a seat. This won't take a minute." Steve walked into the small kitchen and set to making the coffee with excellent freshly ground arabica coffee beans brought in from New Guinea.

While the coffee was perking he rejoined Cal, taking a seat opposite him in one of the armchairs.

"I don't want you to go, Steve," Cal said. "You do a great job. I rely on you and I trust you."

"I appreciate that, Cal. I really do but I can't have one of the McKendricks for me and one bitterly against."

"What about Meredith?"

Steve fought to speak calmly. "What have I got to offer her, Cal? A woman like that."

"Okay, so we can fix things," Cal said. "Do you love her?"

Steve lowered his head. No response.

"Steve?"

When Steve looked up there was misery in his golden eyes. "I was in love with her from the word *go*. Nothing has happened between us, Cal. Just a few kisses."

"One kiss can change a man's life, Steve."

"Tell me about it. It's not as if I've even got a name to offer her. My own mother and Lancaster did that to me."

"That's quite an indictment," Cal said.

"You don't know what it's like, Cal. I know you feel for me but you can't really put yourself in my shoes. You're a McKendrick. That's a proud, pioneering name. You know who you are."

"And you know who *you* are," Cal responded. "You're a top man. Every last person on the station likes and respects you."

"You're leaving out the most important people. Your parents."

"It's quite possible to love one's parents or some member of the family, for that matter, without liking them. I know my father and mother have a certain view of themselves that doesn't jell with the times. Right from the early days Coronation Hill was run more or less on feudal lines. Even Dad's extraordinary attitude to Merri's suitors, and she's had quite a few very serious about her, is feudal. It's the sheer size of the place and the isolation."

"Plus the money, the power and the influence," Steve added harshly. "I really should have taken my mother's maiden name instead of staying with Lockhart. But I guess it's too late to change now."

"Meredith will be tremendously upset if you go."

"I'll think of something," Steve said, his mind jam-packed with mostly crazy ideas. How did a working man win an heiress? A working man with pride?

"I've thought of something," Cal said. "Want to hear it?"

"Just let me get the coffee," Steve said, rising and moving back to the kitchen.

"Thanks," Cal said when Steve returned with a tray wafting

a rich aroma. "What do you think about this? What if I send you to Jingoll?" Jingoll was a McKendrick outstation close in to the McDonnell Ranges in the Territory's Red Centre. "And bring Cash Hammond back here. He's a good bloke. He's not you, but he does the job."

The constriction around Steve's heart eased up slightly. "But wouldn't your father object to that, too, Cal?"

Cal looked untroubled. "Dad's the king of the castle in name only these days, Steve. You know that. *I* run the chain. If I say I'm sending you to Jingoll, Dad will accept it."

"And I never get to see Meredith?" Steve drank his coffee too hot.

"That's up to the two of you, Steve. Merri has a sizeable trust fund."

"God, Cal!" Steve set his mug down so hard it might have been a hammer on an anvil.

"Hear me out," Cal said, holding up a hand. "I'm well aware of your scruples, Steve. All I'm saying is Meredith has the freedom to do what she likes."

"But if she came to me then your parents would give up on her?" Steve met Cal's eyes directly.

"It all translates into choices, Steve. We all have to make our own choices in life."

When Cal returned to the homestead an hour later he went in search of his sister. He needed to tell her what had transpired between him and Steve. Steve moving away from Coronation Hill was an undoubted loss for the station, but a plus for Jingoll. He didn't know what Meredith would think of it however. Jingoll was around eight hundred miles away, the distance between Darwin in the Top End and Alice Springs in the Red Centre being close to a thousand miles. He entered through one of the rear doors of the house, hearing voices coming from down the hallway. As he drew nearer to his father's study he recognised the voices. His mother and Gina were having a discussion. Ordinarily he would have let the sound of his boots announce his arrival, but this time for some reason he trod very quietly along the thick Persian runner, hesitating a few feet from the open doorway.

"So that's how it was done?" Gina was saying, her voice resonating with what Cal thought was quiet resignation.

"Something had to be done," his mother snapped back. "My son was to marry his childhood sweetheart. They were as good as engaged even before that unfortunate holiday."

"So that was the plan," Gina continued as though she was scarcely listening to his mother. "Your sister—a most convincing, beautiful society lady—told me Cal was to marry the girl the entire family loved. It had been known for ages. Sadly for me, I was little more than a bachelor's last fling before Cal tied the knot. A few months on he would be settling down to a splendid marriage—one made in Heaven."

"And so it was!" Jocelyn responded, her tone showing not a skerrick of remorse.

Again Gina didn't sound as if she were listening. It seemed more like she was simply speaking her thoughts aloud. "So you and your sister came up with a plan. She told Cal—who trusted her implicitly—and why not? I saw how sweet and loving she was with him—that I had gone to her, begging her to have me spirited off the island. She was a powerful lady. I was in awe of her. I was so young, the product of an ordinary working-class family. I thought your family lived on a scale I couldn't even imagine. The owner of the island was your sister's good friend. She could do anything. So the two of you concocted the story that I had confessed to her I had given my promise to marry *my* childhood sweetheart. My *fictional* childhood sweetheart. My father was a control freak, Mrs McKendrick. Something like you. I had no boyfriend. Then your sister told Cal I'd become panicked by the situation I found myself in. I had got myself in so deep I wanted only to run away. I was already promised to a young man my father approved of. I remember the exact words she used to me. She seemed so kind, so wise and mature, trying to prevent me from making a fool of myself, but she was playing me for the naive girl I was. *'My dear child, you do realise my nephew is very far above you?'"*

"True, too true!" Jocelyn answered so strongly. Cal winced. "Only by then it was too late. You were already pregnant."

"How could I possibly regret it?" Gina said. "Nothing was easy. My father was so devastated by my fall from grace, he banished me from our home. But I had Cal's son, my beloved Robbie. It may not be what you want, Mrs McKendrick, but Cal and I will be married very soon. Our son is the most important person in the world to us. If you wish to hold on to your son's love it might be in *your* best interest to turn over a new leaf."

There was a shocked silence, then his mother's well-bred voice rising in outrage. "You're advising me, are you?"

Cal judged it high time to make his appearance. He stood framed in the open doorway of the study, trying to keep calm if only on the surface. His mother was wearing her famous pearls. She was seated behind the huge partner's desk that was singularly free of paper work. Meredith, the unsung heroine, took care of all that with her usual quiet efficiency. Gina was standing in front of the desk, with her back to him.

His mother saw him first, her skin draining of all colour. "Cal, how long have you been there?" she quavered.

Gina spun around. Her face, too, betrayed shock. "Cal, we never heard you."

He closed the distance between them, folding an arm around

her. "For once I was eavesdropping. I should do it more often, especially with so many dishonest people about."

Gina's sigh was ragged. "We didn't mean for you to hear anything." She had been trying to effect a private understanding with her future mother-in-law, not drag Cal into it.

"I did tell you to shut the door," Jocelyn snapped, some colour returning to her face. As ever she was determined on braving it out.

"I'm sorry. I should have, but you rather upset me…"

Jocelyn sucked in a breath. "And I'm *not* upset?"

"If you are you deserve to be, Mother," Cal told her bluntly. "You and dear Aunt Lorinda. Just goes to show what a fool I was back then. I *trusted* her. She was family. She'd never shown me anything but love. She's a wonderful actress, too. I was sucked in good and proper."

"Exactly what she wanted," Gina said bleakly. "I believed her, too."

"Let's be very clear here," Jocelyn interrupted, a frown between her eyes, "Lorinda's only motivation was love and concern. She didn't want you, Cal, to make a terrible mistake."

"The terrible mistake was getting engaged to poor Kym. The fact is the two of you conspired to ruin my relationship with Gina," Cal said with a hard condemnatory note Jocelyn had never heard in his voice before. "I won't forget!"

"But, Calvin, we did what we thought best." Jocelyn threw up her hands. "You were set to marry Kym. She was just right for you. I was very grateful to Lorinda for letting me know what was happening on that island. It might be hard to believe now, Gina, but Lorinda quite liked you. She thought you very beautiful and clever, but unfortunately not one of us. She was seriously worried that you may have got hurt."

Gina gave a brittle laugh. "I did get seriously hurt, Mrs McKendrick."

"Please don't let's overlook the damage done to me," Cal broke in, his expression severe. "I'm only just getting to know my son. Robbie is only just getting to know his father. Or did the three of you think it was all *women's* business?" He turned his head to stare Gina down.

Gina didn't answer. Jocelyn sat stricken under her son's weight of judgement.

"What, no replies?" Cal asked, curtly. "No, sorrow, no remorse?"

Jocelyn delicately licked her chiselled lips. They were bone-dry. "Robert is a splendid little fellow." She offered like it was some sort of olive branch. "A true McKendrick. I'm sure the two of us will become great friends. Your father is already very proud of him, Cal. Robert is a beautiful child."

"You would never have laid eyes on him, only Merri happened to see that article about Gina in a paper," Cal pointed out coldly. "It was Merri who drew my attention to it. We have her to thank for bringing Robert into our lives."

"Fate sometimes takes steps to put things right," Gina murmured, lifting her drooping head.

"So where does that leave us?" Jocelyn asked.

Cal clipped off his answer. "It leaves us with the hope *you'll* take a good long look at yourself, Mum. You cross Gina, you cross me. Gina is to be my wife. She's the mother of my son. I love you—you know that—but I won't tolerate your trying to destroy the life the two of us want for our son. You messed up once. You're not allowed to do it again."

Cal turned about and stalked from the room, leaving the two women staring at one another. It would have been an exaggeration to say they were suddenly allies but they both felt the weight of his deep abiding anger.

* * *

Robbie, running around the ground floor, in an ecstasy of exploration, found Jocelyn some time later in the big room with all the plants. It was a dazzling world for a small boy used only to the confines of a two-bedroom apartment. In the room where his grandmother was, there were *trees* that nearly reached the ceiling. There were lovely big fat pots taller than he was, like the pots full of golden canes Aunt Rosa had in her garden. Huge hanging baskets were suspended from the ceiling, tumbling masses of beautiful ferns and flowers. He had never seen so many flowers in his life.

Mummy always had flowers in the apartment. He and Aunt Rosa used to go out into the garden late afternoon and pick some for her before she came home. Mummy liked lilies. There were beds and beds of lilies out in the garden, which seemed to him more like the Botanical Gardens Mummy used to take him to. He had never seen anything in his short life like this place called Coronation Hill. Not just the great big castle, but all the little houses and long dormitories for the stockmen grouped around it. There were no streets or streetlights, no highways, on Coronation; no tall buildings, no buses or trains, nor lots of cars whizzing up and down. There were no coffee shops and restaurants, none of the shops where Mummy normally went to buy things. Instead there were planes and a helicopter, lots of heavy machinery, thousands and thousands of really marvellous-looking cattle, emus, kangaroos—he'd heard *crocodiles*—zillions of birds and best of all *horses*. He couldn't wait until the special pony his daddy had ordered for him would arrive. But above all there was this enormous, empty land! It spread out to the horizons and they had it all to themselves! That was amazing! Coronation Hill was an enchanted kingdom. And it was his home.

"Hello, Nana!" he carolled, delighted to see her. His grandmother was sitting quietly with her back to him so he ran around the front of her, stopping short in dismay, "Oh, Nanna, you're *crying!*"

Jocelyn tried very hard to stem the flow. She had been sitting there coming to terms with what was going on in her life. It seemed to her she had never been so alone, darn near ostracised. Of course she was to blame. Her attitude was so negative. Even she could see that. Ewan was very upset with her. Their argument the night before had badly affected her. Cal, her beloved son, was starting to think badly of her. Of course she was jealous. *Go on, admit it!* She had been the Number One woman in her son's life. She wasn't any more. That was hard to take, especially for a possessive woman like her. A winner all her life it seemed to her all of a sudden she could finish up a big loser if she persisted with the hard line she had taken. Maybe there was something dreadfully wrong with her? The only answer was to express an abject apology directly to Gina, her soon-to-be daughter-in-law and suggest they start again.

"Nanna?" Robbie asked uncertainly, worried his grandmother might be sick or something.

Jocelyn came out of her unhappy reverie. "Just a few little tears, darling boy. Nothing for you to worry about. I'm fine now. What have you been up to?" she asked, trying to speak brightly.

Robbie moved close to her, putting his elbows in her lap and staring into her face. "Why are you so sad?"

Jocelyn gave a funny little groan. "How can I be sad with you around?" She gave him a lovely trembling smile.

Robbie leaned upwards and kissed her on the cheek. "It's so wonderful here, Nanna. I *love* it. It's my home now, isn't it?"

"It certainly is," Jocelyn responded, the icebergs that had all but held her heart fast, starting to melt away. "Coronation Hill is where you belong."

"And Mummy?" Robbie asked earnestly, taking her hand. "Don't you think she's beautiful?"

Jocelyn saw a far-reaching question in her grandson's highly intelligent eyes. *Her* eyes, wasn't that remarkable?

"Yes, darling, I do," she said, allowing herself to be drawn to her feet. "Mummy is very beautiful and she's raised you beautifully. She should be very proud. We're going to have the greatest time ever on the wedding day. I expect you want to be page boy?"

"Page boy, what's that?" Robbie looked up at her a shade anxiously.

"Come along with me and I'll show you," Jocelyn said. "I can show you photographs of your daddy when he was page boy at several big society weddings. That was when he was around four or five. He said he was too old thereafter and refused. Aunty Merri was flower girl at lots of weddings. It's all in the albums."

"Please show me," Robbie said with the greatest interest. "Are there photos of you, Nanna? Mummy said you would have been a fairy-tale bride?"

Jocelyn's gratified smile flashed out. She bent and kissed the top of her grandson's glossy head. "Oh, I was, my darling," she said. "I can show you. I used to have hair like your mummy's. It flowed all the way down my back."

"Like Rapunzel?" Robbie giggled.

"Rapunzel didn't stand a chance!" Jocelyn joyfully squeezed his hand.

CHAPTER SEVEN

MEREDITH rode until she and the gelding were close to exhaustion. It was the gelding's condition far more than her own that had her reining in at the creek, a place that she loved, all the more so now, because it was the place she and Steven had first acknowledged what they could mean to each other. The lead up had been slow—the going was tough—but finally when left alone together caution had given way to feelings of the heart. She just knew in her bones Steven wouldn't stay after the harshness of the way her father had spoken to him. He had insulted Steven in the worst possible way. It was so cruel, so unfair. Steven was the victim of the illicit affair between Gavin Lancaster and his mother. Steven was blameless. Yet he had been saddled with a burden almost too heavy to carry for most of his life.

Meredith sat down on the bank beneath the willowy melaleucas, with hundreds of little wildflowers, purple with yellow, black-spotted throats, growing all around the base of the sweet sapped trees. Above her, she could see chinks of the smouldering blue sky. There could be a late tropical thunderstorm though a cooling breeze had sprung up. It was moving its fingers through her hair and quelling the heat in her skin. A pair of brolgas were standing on their long legs amid the reeds at the water's edge. Brolgas mated for life. These days humans weren't taking sacred

vows all that seriously. When she married she wanted it to b
for ever.

She thought about the way Steven had kissed her; the way h
held her; the depth of feeling he had transmitted to her throug
his mouth and his hands. Yet she had been much more certai
yesterday that he loved her than she was today. At least *in lov*
with her. That very first kiss had been to her, the start of som
thing big. She asked herself if it had really been that way for hir

A flight of pygmy-geese with their glossy green upper par
and breast bands had arrived, hovering above the mirror-clea
surface of the water as though admiring their reflections. On th
opposite bank brilliantly coloured parrots were alighting i
the trees with wonderful flashes of emerald, deepest sapphir
scarlet, yellow, orange. Australia was famous for the numbe
and varieties of its parrots. Almost certainly they had originate
on the ancient southern continent of Gondwana. For once th
sight of them didn't give her the usual pleasure. At that mome
she felt as though all pleasure had been drained out of her.

She *had* to speak to Steven.

Back home at the stables, she turned the gelding over to on
of the stable hands to take care of, and then she cut through th
home grounds, narrowly dodging her uncle and Rosa who ap
peared to crave one another's company. She made for the sta
quarters beyond the home compound, encountering no one alon
the way. She prayed Steven would be at the bungalow even if h
were packing to leave. It amazed her now, the amount of inte
ference in her affairs she had tolerated from her father. She ha
to stop living that kind of life. But it also struck her Steven wa
the first man she was fully prepared to fight for. She had take
a long time to truly fall in love. Maybe that was it.

She was running up the short flight of timber steps whe
Steven faced her at the door.

"Hi!" he said, his strong face impassive.

"May I come in?" She felt incredibly nervous.

"Sure." He stood away from the door. "You look tired." There were shadows beneath her beautiful, intensely blue eyes.

"I couldn't sleep. How could I what with everything that's going on."

"Would you like some coffee?" he asked. "Cal was here. I made him some, but I'm ready to make fresh."

She shook her head. "No, don't bother unless you want some. I haven't seen Cal. I've been for a ride because I was in the mood for a darn good gallop. Trying to clear my head. So what did you and Cal decide?"

"Sit down, please." It struck him she looked more fragile than he had ever seen her.

Meredith sank into an armchair, looking around her. The bungalow was comfortably and attractively furnished. Steven had kept it immaculately. No one could describe him as a careless man. "Two years later and this is the first time I've ever been inside your bungalow." She gave a brittle laugh. "Doesn't that say something?"

"It says you're Ms McKendrick and I'm the overseer," he clipped off.

She swallowed on her dry throat. "May I have a cold drink if you've got it?" she asked.

"Mineral water?" He glanced back at her, wanting desperately to take her into his arms. Determined not to.

"That'll be fine." She clasped her hands together. "Well, how did you end up?" she asked when he returned. "I must know."

"How did we end up?" He put the frosted glass into her hand, his shapely mouth compressed.

"Steven, please answer me," she begged. "You know how much I care about you."

"Enough to take off with me today?" He stood staring down at her, his expression taut and challenging.

Her heart jumped. "What, on the freight plane?" *Could* she, would she? What could she throw in a bag? Where would they go? Their flight from Coronation would be the talk of the Outback.

"Yes," Steve said. "You look mighty nervous."

"But it's a stunning suggestion, isn't it, Steven?" Her sapphire eyes pleaded with him to understand.

"You'd come if you loved me."

She thought, *Is that right? Is that what I should be prepared to do?* "I don't know, Steven." She shook her head from side to side. "I just don't know." She needed a little time.

"It's okay," he replied, as if he never for a moment expected her to say yes. "I'll put you out of your misery. Cal has made the decision for me. I'm to go to Jingoll and Cash Hammond is to come here."

"What?" For a moment she thought she would burst into tears. But shouldn't she be used to hiding her feelings by now? "Jingoll is outside Alice Springs."

"So?" His heart rose a little at her evident distress.

"How do I get to see you?" she demanded emotionally. "I wanted to learn to fly the plane but Dad wouldn't hear of it. Even Cal couldn't shift him. What am I supposed to do, drive all darned day and all darned night?"

"You've got money." He shrugged, pretending indifference to her plight. "You could call up a plane just like that! Fix it with Jim Pitman today. He could fly you down to me. Stay a week or two." *To hell with it! Make it easy for her to make the break.*

"Do you love me, Steven?" she asked with her heart in her eyes. "Or are you just a little bit *in* love with me? We don't entirely know one another."

"No, we don't," he replied soberly. He could see the way

things were shaping up. Put to the test she was getting cold feet. And why not? He had no reputation to protect. *She* was Meredith McKendrick. "I should be finishing off packing," he said, just short of dismissively.

A tight hand closed over Meredith's heart. "Maybe we can meet again in a little while?" She stood up, trying unsuccessfully to pin his eyes.

"Why not? There are always rodeos, bush races and what not."

Her head dropped. "I'm sorry, Steven. So sorry for everything." She went to move past him to the door, fighting down a storm of tears, only he suddenly caught her to him, golden eyes glittering. He forced her head back into the crook of his arm, his mouth coming down on hers. Passionate. Heated. Punishing.

When he released her she put a hand to her breast. Her heart was hammering unnaturally.

"Just something to remember me by," Steven offered tonelessly.

Steve headed almost directly south to the McKendrick holding that was situated close to the fantastically coloured McDonnell Ranges of the Red Centre. Here the landscape was as different from the tropical north as it could be. The Red Centre seemed as old as time itself, the mystique of the place amazing. Jingoll ran Brahmins, beautiful cattle crossed with the best Queensland Brahmans and going further back, fine American Brahmin stock. Jingoll's Brahmins were well-known in the industry.

The change-over went remarkably smoothly, Steve assuming the top job of manager caused no problems whatever with the staff. Everyone knew he had been the overseer at the McKendrick flagship, Coronation Hill, but the rumour was, as Cal McKendrick's man, he had been sent to make Jingoll an even bigger outfit than it was. That was okay by all. Steve Lockhart might be young but if he'd been overseer on Coronation, he really knew what he was about.

Steve set about proving it from day one. The best way he could cope was to bury himself in hard work. Work shifted the burden of his wretchedness a little. But he thought about her every minute of the day. Then again he had to admit Jingoll gave him a breathing space, while he tried to think how best to go about the difficult task of wooing an heiress which was far more a hindrance than a help. During his first few weeks he made several trips to Alice Springs or "The Alice" as everyone called it. The Alice almost in the dead centre of the continent was a big supply depot for the outlying cattle stations, mines and aboriginal settlements. In addition to being an important commercial centre it was also an enormously popular tourist spot for visitors from around Australia and overseas. The Alice was the jumping off point for the Red Centre's great monuments and beauty spots; *Uluru, Kata Tjuta, Mount Connor, the Devil's Marbles, Rainbow Valley, King's Canyon* and the extraordinary *Palm Valley,* a sight Steve found staggering, blooming as it did in all its tropical splendour in the middle of the red desert.

On that particular day Steve having completed station business allowed himself a couple of cold beers and a big wedge of Mediterranean sandwich, a freshly baked round loaf stuffed with half a dozen delicious ingredients, before he made the long drive back to the outstation. He was sitting at the bar counter alongside a chatty local called Pete, when an old fellow with the long grey hair of an ancient prophet and a matching grey beard burst through the pub doors jabbering something with his mouth wide-open. Despite that, his voice was so agitated, so high and reedy, most of those in the pub couldn't make out what he was carrying on about.

"What did he say?" Steve asked, not really interested. Pete was polishing off his own sandwich with gusto. It was seriously good.

"Hang on!" Pete swung around in his chair. "That's old Barney. Should be Balmy. He's a terminal alcoholic. Has been for the last forty years." Barney was still into his high decibel hollering but it took a moment for everyone to work out what he was on about. By the time everyone did, the humming bar inhabited by tourists, locals and stockmen having a day off in town, shut down to a stunned silence.

"Struth!" said Pete as though someone important had just died without warning. As, indeed, they had.

The pub owner, ponderously moving his huge frame and smoothing back his remaining strands of sandy hair, came from behind the bar. "News is just in, folks," he announced. "No need to mind Barney though he got it right for once. I have to tell you Gavin Lancaster, his son, the station overseer and another passenger, not yet identified, have been killed in transit to Darwin. Their Cessna with Lancaster at the controls went down some thirty kilometres north-east of the ranges. Apparently there was no emergency call, nothing. The wreckage was spotted by the Flying Doctor on a routine flight. So there it is! Lancaster is dead, when most of us thought he'd live to be a hundred."

Pete immediately swung to face Steven, studying him with unblinking light blue eyes almost too big for their sockets. "God, mate, that's your dad, isn't it?" he burst out. "Isn't Lancaster your dad? Hell, you're the living spit of him. I spotted it right away. I tell yah, mate, I'm shocked. *Shocked!*"

Steve didn't say anything. He couldn't trust himself to open his mouth even if he could find his voice. Instead he had the urge to bolt. As always he had been aware of the curious stares coming his way ever since he had entered the pub. It happened all the time. What could he possibly tell this guy, Pete, he didn't already know?

"Do you think there are things like justice in this world, mate," Pete put the question to him in a philosophical kind of way.

"What's your point?" Finally Steve managed to find his tongue, though even to him it sounded like a croak.

"My point, Stevo, is this!" said Pete. "And remember you got it from me. They've always said Lancaster was scared of nobody—but maybe he was a little bit scared of the Almighty? I know I am. It could well be Lancaster decided to do the right thing at long last and put you in his will."

Steve wrenched up a sad, bitter laugh. "He didn't know me." He stood up wanting to get out of the pub as fast as possible. For one thing everyone was now staring his way. That's what happened when you had the Lancaster brand on your forehead.

"I dunno, mate," Pete said, shaking his head, "my feeling is you're being a bit hard on yourself. I recognised you right off. Didn't say nuthin' then, o'course. Didn't want a punch in the nose. Only jokin', mate. You look a real good guy. Different from old Lancaster, God rest his soul," he added piously. "My bet is, you might be hearin' from his lawyers yet."

"*You've* got a better chance of hearing from them, Pete," Steve said, and moved off.

When he got back to Jingoll homestead, several voice messages were waiting for him. All of them related to the crash of the Lancasters' plane. The news had circulated through the Outback with the speed of a high-priority cyclone. One message was from Cal saying he was sorry so many lives had been lost. No more. The family would be attending the Lancaster funerals as a matter of course. These Outback courtesies and marks of respect were understood.

Well, the high and mighty McKendricks might be there, but I sure as hell won't, Steve thought, though the news had powerfully upset him. Lost lives he supposed. Light aircraft coming down in the Outback was a fact of life. One of the dead was his biological father, another his half brother, Brad. Even so he wouldn't be attending any funeral. The family had never had any use for him. He had no use for them, either.

But there he was wrong.

Once again Fate had made the decision to step in.

The day of the funerals was one of scorching heat with banks of grape coloured clouds shot through with streaks of living green, piled up on the horizon. No one took much notice. Outback skies could turn on truly ominous displays without one drop of rain falling. The heat and the threatening sky didn't prevent mourners from all over the country making their pilgrimage to the Channel Country in the extreme South West pocket of the State of Queensland. This was the stronghold of the cattle kings. The select band of families and pastoral companies ran the nation's greatest concentration of beef cattle in their unique, riverine desert. The Lancaster fortress, *Euroka,* an aboriginal word for *blazing sun* was the flagship, but the Lancaster chain like the McKendrick empire spread its life lines through adjoining States.

Gavin Lancaster's two daughters, Catherine and Sarah, both in their early forties, tall, elegant women, stood tearless, but their faces spoke of controlled grief. Standing with them at the graveside was their half brother, Steven. It was Catherine, the elder sister, who had persuaded Steven to attend. She had been adamant he should finally take his rightful place by their side. It was something Steve found enormously touching and, yes, *healing.* The family resemblance between all three siblings was so strong it made it much easier for them to identify with one another. The husbands were unable to attend so Steven stood in for them both. One was a brilliant economist at present a speaker at an overseas conference; the other a cardiologist with a very tight schedule.

Much had happened in the week since the fatal plane crash.

The man who appeared to have ignored Steve's existence for all of his life had left him by virtue of his elder half brother's death a sixty percent controlling interest in Lancaster Holdings. It had been a shock on a monumental scale. Steve had gone on to learn from the family's high-powered lawyer, who strangely enough had looked and acted more like a kindly parish priest, that Gavin Lancaster had secretly supported him for most of his life. Lancaster had made it possible for him to attend his prestigious school. Lancaster, too, working behind the scenes, had been instrumental in those early days, when Steve was fresh out of school, in getting him placed on a top station.

There were more shocks in store. Steve learned Lancaster had kept copies of his school reports and his sporting achievements along with a whole batch of photographs. Steve in his wildest imaginings had never conceived of such a thing. Looking through the photographs, he'd had to swallow many times on the hard lump in his throat. So the man Steve had spent most of his life despising had looked out for him all along, though Gavin Lancaster had chosen to live his life without his *other* son.

Perhaps his wife wouldn't have tolerated me beneath their roof, Steve thought. Who would know?

Steve could hear the Lancaster lawyer's voice in his head. "I never truly understood why your father did what he did, Steven. You're obviously a fine young man, but he tried to make up for it in the end. You won't have any problem whatever with the daughters. They're women of depth and character. Both married now to outstanding men with no connection to the industry. Their interests lie elsewhere, so you'll have a free hand to run Euroka. Cal McKendrick speaks very highly of you, so you're up to it. Needless to say my firm is ready to support you in any way we can." He had smiled encouragingly as he took off his glasses. "Let me be the first to offer my congratulations. It's your father's wish that you be known from henceforth as Steven Lancaster. And perfectly right it is, too!"

Rags to riches! Steve thought. But riches couldn't be measured against the lifelong abandonment of a father. So far as he was concerned they could take it all away in exchange for the chance of having belonged.

Afterwards at the reception at Euroka homestead, Steven found he couldn't have been treated better. Amazing what being handed a grand inheritance could do, he thought cynically. Some of the mourners even greeted him with a touch of reverence. Overnight a lot of power had been put into his hands. He and his half sisters made their way around the two large reception rooms briefly greeting people with a few words and a handshake. It might have been kind of crazy, but Steve felt he was supporting Cate and Sarah, far more than they were supporting him. But then it was obvious they had loved their father no matter what his faults and they had certainly loved their brother who, they had told Steve, had been overwhelmed by the thought of his future responsibilities.

"You see, Brad wasn't a cattleman," Cate had told him with tears in her eyes. *"The thought of stepping into Dad's shoes used to terrify him. Brad really wanted a quiet life. Now he's got it. None quieter than the grave."*

Steve turned to find himself face-to-face with the McKendricks. To anyone watching—and a great many were— it would have appeared the Lancaster heir was being comforted and consoled by close family friends.

Ewan McKendrick even got a little carried away with his words of reconciliation, Jocelyn McKendrick offered Steve her sincere condolences when she really meant congratulations. "I'm sure Catherine and Sarah are going to depend on you a lot!" She gave him a little encouraging pat on the arm.

Now I'm *one of them!* Steve thought, just so tired of all the hypocrisy.

Cal and Gina came to him, saying exactly the kind of thing he wanted to hear. When they moved off he was left alone with Meredith.

"Isn't life amazing?" He spoke with great irony.

"Maybe that's why it's so interesting?" she said, staring up at him, soaking him in. From somewhere he had found a beautifully tailored black suit, pristine white business shirt, obligatory black tie. Probably one of his half sisters had organised it, getting it in from the city. It fitted perfectly. He looked extraordinarily handsome and strangely daunting. Almost another person. "How are you *really?*" she asked, striving not to feel rebuffed.

"Well, most importantly I'm *rich.* Even your mother and father are prepared to accept me. Let bygones be bygones and all the rest." He glanced over her head to where Cal and Gina were standing at the centre of a small group. "Cal and his Gina make a beautiful couple. Where's young Robbie?"

"He's at home with Rosa and Uncle Ed. After ten years on his own Uncle Ed looks set to remarry. Rosa has reminded him of all the lovely things he had forgotten."

"Good. I like your uncle Ed. He deserves to rediscover some happiness. Cal and Gina working things out?" Gina, as if sensing she was being spoken about, suddenly turned to give them a little smile and a wave.

Meredith waved back. "They *appear* to be, yet I feel both of them are struggling with a lot of hurt. We've since found out there was a conspiracy going on to keep them apart. My mother and my aunt Lorinda I'm sorry to say."

"Why doesn't that surprise me?"

His tone stung.

"You'll be getting your invitation to the wedding," Meredith continued, very uncomfortable beneath his searing gaze.

"I expect I will. *Now.*"

"I know how you must feel." It was a great strain being with him in this mood.

"You don't know how I feel, Meredith." The sight of her was playing havoc with his nerves. He wanted to haul her into his arms and scream at her, as well. "How could you? You look lovely, by the way. Black suits you." With her long arched neck and her hair pulled back into some sort of roll she was as graceful as a swan.

Meredith stared over to where her brother and Gina were standing. "Cal wants to take us home, Steven," she said, aware of the flight plans. "I made a mistake coming here. The family is represented. I'm sorry."

"You *didn't* make a mistake, Meredith," he said crisply, his manner changing. "We have to talk."

She looked up at him startled. "About what? You're in a strange mood."

"Why wouldn't I be? I've had so many shocks this past week I scarcely know how to handle myself."

"You look perfectly in command to me. Your half sisters genuinely care about you. I've spoken to both of them."

"They're lovely women." His expression momentarily softened. "I'll never forget it was they who approached me. Far too much of my life has been wasted."

"You can change all that, Steven," she said gently.

"Sure!" His tone was falsely expansive. "I have the solution to all my problems. I have money, position, the running of one of the country's legendary cattle stations. I can even get the girl I want. I can't buy her, of course. She's got money of her own. But I'm pretty sure if I talk to her dad, he'll give me the green light."

Her hands were trembling. "Do you think that's all you need, my father's approval?" She threw up her gently determined chin.

"Meredith, did you think I was talking about *you?*" he asked suavely. "Wait and see if I don't make the most eligible list like Cal. There won't even be a scandal. The media will turn it all into a biblical tale. Prodigal son comes home. All anyone cares about is *money* and who's got it!"

She pressed her palms together to steady her hands. "On the contrary, *I* don't care about money, Steven. I don't think I even care about you any more. You're eaten up with bitterness."

He shook his head at her, a demonic sparkle in his golden eyes. "While *you're* a rich young woman who hasn't yet learned to stand on her own two feet."

Sparks rose into the air around them. "I'm surprised you saw anything in me in the first place," she said. "I'll say goodbye, Steven. I hope you have a good life. I mean that."

"How sweet!" He surprised her by catching her wrist, locking his fingers about it. "You leave now and you'll never see me again." He bent to her, speaking very quietly.

The strangeness of his manner was undermining her. "Surely you can't be asking me to stay?"

"I'm *telling* you to stay." Now his voice was full of authority. "Did you really think you could get away from me as easily as that?" He drew her so close to his side, its significance couldn't be lost on the room.

"You're mad!" There was no way she could break away without causing a scene.

"That's too ridiculous. I'm nothing of the kind. Pop along now and tell the family you're going to stay over. Tell them I have lots to tell you. Tell them your new life begins *now.*"

* * *

MARGARET WAY 145

It was inevitable at some point Cal and Gina would encounter Kym. Sad occasion or not Cal could see the simmering jealousy just below the surface of Kym's murmured greetings, so civil and proper. Cal knew she took not the slightest pleasure in meeting Gina, but she was doing a fairly good job of hiding it. Though not from Gina he fancied. Gina was extraordinarily intuitive. Kym was busy assessing her from head to toe, working very hard to find a flaw.

You won't find one, Cal thought, wishing all the hurt would seep out of him, believing it would take time. His big question was, why when Gina had found herself pregnant, did she not try to contact him? Even had he been engaged to Kym—never mind that hadn't happened—but even *if*—he would have broken his engagement and married her. He had put the question to her heavy heartedly and she had recoiled.

"My worst fear was you would take my baby from me."

"How could you possibly have thought such a thing?"

"Because I was scared. Scared of you. Scared of your family. Why are you trying to blame me?"

The sad truth was, he *did.*

As for Kym, desperately unhappy after the break-up of her engagement to Cal, she now found herself desperately unhappy once more. It showed in her paleness which she hoped would be interpreted as sadness. She had truly believed—with Jocelyn's encouragement—she only had to bide her time and Cal would come to his senses, accepting she was the best possible choice for him. Now he had presented them all with the object of his mad passion from years back. Not only that, a ready made heir, who according to a besotted Jocelyn was "the image of Cal." In one fell swoop Cal McKendrick, the man Kym had fixated on for so many good years of her life was lost to her. She had ceased to exist for him. She could see it in his eyes as they rested on her, the outsider.

Even as she entertained such thoughts, Kym was murmuring to this woman who had stolen her heart's desire from her. "I do hope we're going to be friends, Gina. May I wish you both much joy." It was a lovely little speech and it tripped sweetly off her tongue. She would *hate* it to be barred from Coronation Hill. Hate it still more not to retain Cal as her friend.

"So that was your ex-fiancée?" Gina remarked quietly as Kym drifted away. "She still loves you." Her voice softened with pity. Gina knew all too well the pain of loss.

Cal couldn't be drawn. He had caught sight of some people he wanted Gina to meet. "Kym will find the right guy to make her happy," he said. "I certainly hope so. She's wasted years of her life on me." He began to steer Gina across the crowded room.

First, Kym has to forget you, Gina thought. She doubted she and Kym would ever become friends. Thank God for Meredith! It made Gina happy to know she had Meredith supporting her. Their friendship had progressed rapidly. Meredith was a lovely person. She deserved happiness, a full life. Gina had the presentiment all roads led to Steven Lockhart, or Steven Lancaster as he was now known. She'd had to bite down hard on her lip when Cal's parents had offered Steven their condolences. The acquisition of land and a proud pioneering name really did make extraordinary things happen, she thought.

CHAPTER EIGHT

BY MIDAFTERNOON the last of the mourners had left the station in their private planes, charter planes, helicopters, trucks, one bus and all manner of four-wheel drives. Catherine and Sarah were among them. The sisters had spent a few hours of the afternoon discussing Lancaster family matters with Steven, grief-stricken about the deaths of their father and brother, but enormously relieved, even jubilant at the back of their minds a Lancaster would take over the running of Euroka and its several outstations.

"Lord knows what would have happened had Fate not brought you into the family frame, Steven," Catherine said.

Both women were anxious to return to their children; each had two girls, not present at the funerals, because the sisters hadn't deemed it advisable to uproot them from school, and if the truth be known, their father and brother had shown little interest in any of them. Both sisters put that down to the fact they were all girls. It was a sad fact of life—one that Meredith could attest to—some fathers had little use for their girl children.

"Fortunately *our* girls' fathers adore them," Cate assured them.

Steve's response was immediate and sincere. "Well, I want to meet them at the earliest opportunity."

"Oh, they'll love you!" Sarah had turned to him, blinking tears out of her golden-brown eyes.

Another prophecy that turned out perfectly true.

Meredith and Steve returned to the empty homestead in a near silence. Both of them had been treading around one another almost on tiptoe. It was amazing how greatly humans tortured themselves, suffering in silence, often unnecessarily, devising strategies for containing emotions, strangely frightened to reveal what was really in their hearts lest they be met by rejection. Love was such a terrible ache.

Meredith went to stand at the balustrade staring out at the horizon. The sky was piling higher, ever higher incandescent storm clouds, great plumes of purple, indigo, black, slivers of silver. Their depths shot through with the crimson rays of the sinking sun. It was a fantastic sight against the burning red of the pyramids of sand that lay to the north and the south-west of the station. The mirage was abroad, busy playing its usual tricks. Silhouettes of tall, slender trees stood out amid the wavy silver lines. Little stick people ran about in the somnolent heat and in the roughest driest areas blue lagoons glittered like polished mirrors, overshadowed by thickets of palms. These were the phantom pools and water holes the explorers of old had been tricked into trekking towards with no hope of ever reaching their destination. If only they had met up with some aboriginal tribe, Meredith thought. Aboriginals knew the exact location of wells and springs in the most forbidding country. She knew of many pioneer lives that had been saved by the kindness of the tribal people, including her own family.

The heat had increased not diminished with the closing hours of the day. It was difficult to believe such an extraordinary celestial display might not amount to a powerful electrical storm. At least it might clear the air, she thought.

Doug Winstone, the station overseer, was making his way towards the homestead. He had a curious rolling gait, the result of a serious injury some years back when an enraged bull had gored his leg.

"I'll go and have a few words with him," Steven called.

"Righto, and please tell him to thank Julie once again." Meredith lifted a hand to Doug who doffed his dusty hat.

"Will do."

It was Doug's wife, Julie, who had cooked and cleaned for the homestead over a number of years, but she and Doug had never been asked to take up residence in any part of a very large house. Instead, Julie had gone back and forth from the overseer's bungalow. It was she and the other station wives who had served at the funeral reception, although Cate had ordered in the mountain of sandwiches, biscuits and small cakes that had disappeared beneath the mourners' famished onslaught.

She watched the two men talking earnestly, no doubt discussing job priorities. She, herself, had been greeted most respectfully as if everyone on the station expected that she and Steven would make a match of it after an appropriate period of mourning. They looked an odd couple, Steven and Doug. Steven so tall and young man lean, Doug short of stature, top heavy, with a bull neck, powerful shoulders and a barrel chest. He and Steven had reached an understanding right away. It showed in the body language. These were two men who already trusted each other.

She moved back from the balustrade that badly needed repainting. The verandah wrapped the lower floor but not the top floor. She thought that a shame but it could easily be added on. The homestead was a mix of Regency and Victorian architecture. It had symmetry about it, but it was definitely not a welcoming place. All houses had an aura and this house badly needed its aura changing. It was an unremarkable building compared to

Coronation's homestead, but she was certain it could be turned into something far more impressive. The size was there. The interior rooms were all large, with high ceilings, and well proportioned. A lot of charm could be added to the exterior simply with adding some decorative details; certainly a repainting of the shutters on the large sash windows and all the timberwork, columns, balustrading, fretwork, etc. The broad, canopied verandah was very attractive, but the timber columns needed to be wreathed in flowering vines, maybe a beautiful violet-blue to go with the shutters that could be painted darkest green. She knew *exactly* what had to be done, even if she could see it would be a big ongoing job.

They had seen Cate and Sarah off at the airstrip. Neither sister had appeared the least bit surprised she should stay back with Steven. There was only one possible reason for that, Meredith thought. They believed what Doug and Julie Winstone believed; she and Steven were lovers. Her breath came sharp and jagged at the very thought. She felt herself on the very brink of a major turning point in her life, even if it looked as though the two of them were in retreat. It was a travesty of her true feelings.

The two men concluded their conversation. Doug tipped his hat to her once again. She responded with another wave, while Steven strode back to her. How she admired the wide line of his shoulders, the narrow waist, the lean hips.

"What exactly am I doing here?" she asked him as they moved into the unattractive entrance hall when such an area should always be inviting. It was long and fairly narrow with a timber staircase that led to the upper floor set just outside the drawing room. Something else that needed relocating.

"I would have thought that was obvious." Steven spoke with a false nonchalance, thinking all this past week he had been moving in a dream. He, who had always been on the outside, was in overnight. "You're keeping me company. Otherwise you would have gone home with your family."

"I suppose!" She answered coolly enough, when she was all but delirious with anticipation. She was, after all, quite, quite alone with him and she had taken steps to ensure she was safe.

"So this is Euroka homestead," Steve muttered, as they moved into the drawing room. "It's rather a scary old place, isn't it?" He lifted his handsome dark head, staring about him. "That was my dominant impression. It could even be haunted."

Meredith couldn't control a shiver. "It does seem to have a coldness at its heart." She too began to look around her, making changes inside her head. It wouldn't be all that hard to make the room look more natural and inviting simply by pulling down the heavy velvet curtains. Velvet in the Outback! She would introduce cool colours for a start. Maybe citron and white? The drawing room was furnished with a number of fine antique pieces—indeed, to Meredith's eye it looked like a drawing room of the Victorian period—but the spacious room had an air of neglect about it. It even looked dusty though there wasn't a speck of actual dust in sight. Julie Winstone and her helpers had made sure of that. But a home was not complete without the woman at its heart.

Steven's voice broke into her reverie. "No woman!" he said, echoing her own thoughts. "No woman's touch! How long ago was it the girls' mother died? They didn't say and I didn't like to ask."

"Quite early I think. Cate and Sarah are in their early forties. I think their mother died when they were still in their twenties." Meredith fingered the heavy velvet curtains, wanting to give them a good yank. They were stiff with age. "I know both of them married young."

"Probably broke their necks to leave home," Steve observed dryly. "Hell, this is a terrible place. It looks like it's been caught in a time warp."

"It's *your* place now," Meredith reminded him. "Men left alone generally let things slide. The house is shabby, but that can be easily fixed."

"It's not only shabby. It's unnaturally quiet."

Indeed, the only sound was the soft fall of their footsteps on the massive Persian rug. That at least was splendid, all jewelled medallions and floral arabesques. "It knows one era has ended and another has begun," Meredith hazarded, into the deathly quiet.

"Maybe the house doesn't approve of me." Steven had caught sight of his reflection in a tall gilt-framed mirror. It seemed to him he had changed. Maybe it was the sombre funeral clothes Cate had flown in for him. He had never owned such clothes in his life. "Have I changed or is it just me?" He turned to Meredith, a strikingly handsome young man who now had a chance at achieving some measure of greatness.

She didn't have to consider. "Yes, you have."

"In what way?" He didn't know if he liked the sound of that.

"You're a cattle baron now and you're behaving accordingly. Or to put it another way you've been given the opportunity to be your own man."

The corners of his mouth compressed. "It might come as a shock to you, Ms McKendrick but I thought I *was*."

"Oh, please, I didn't mean to offend you." Meredith gave a little grimace. "You know what I mean. Money gives one confidence if nothing else."

"It hasn't given confidence to *you*."

"You want to hurt me back?" Her intensely blue eyes met his.

"I suppose I do." He shrugged, slanting her a half smile. "A little anyway. This place is unnerving me. How am I going to make a home here?"

"You will." Meredith continued to gaze around her. She might have been an interior designer he had called in with all the answers at her fingertips. "Some pieces should be kept, others put into storage. You need new custom-made sofas, new curtains, a cool colour scheme. Maybe the sash windows knocked out and replaced with French doors. One or two Asian pieces wouldn't go astray and an important painting. I like the mix of different styles, don't you? This is just one of those awful days."

"Isn't it just!" He sighed deeply. "I've buried a father and a half brother I never knew. Wouldn't you have thought my half brother at least would have tried to meet me?"

Something in the way he said it brought her perilously close to tears. "You've heard enough about Gavin Lancaster to know he was a strange, hard man, Steven. I'm certain he had great power over his family. He probably ordered them not to make contact. Your existence was no secret, but he had decided to shut you out." Meredith half turned away, quite upset over it.

"At least I now know Cate and Sarah had wanted to meet me." Steven spoke in a gentler voice. "I'm most grateful for that. But things could have been so different. No use talking about that now, of course."

"Fate has stepped in," Meredith said. "You were always meant to come home."

His expression was disbelieving. "You're not saying Euroka is home?" That idea struck him as downright peculiar.

Meredith nodded. "You can't damn your father for everything. At the end he gave you back your heritage. Your job is to keep it safe."

Steve picked up a smallish bronze sculpture of a horse and rider, balancing it in the palm of his hand. It was a work of art. "He didn't know he was going to die. He didn't know his son and heir would die with him."

"Fate, Steven," Meredith repeated. "We have to leave it at that."

They were at the far end of the drawing room, moving into

the adjoining room when Steve asked, "Are you sure there's not someone following us?" The hairs on the back of his neck were standing up.

"You've got a lot of imagination for a tough-minded man," Meredith countered briskly, when she really felt like grabbing his hand.

"And I'm not on my own. *You* can feel it, too," he accused her. He knew if he touched her he wouldn't let her go.

"I wish I couldn't," Meredith confessed. "I don't fancy sleeping on my own."

"Who said you had to?" He gave her a down-bent golden glance. He was overwhelmed by her loveliness yet he felt an immense pressure on him to behave well. He didn't lack commitment, but the last thing he wanted to do was panic her.

"*I* said. I'm here on the understanding you keep your distance." Deliberately, she walked ahead of him, in retreat again. They were in a smaller room, a sort of parlour. It was enormously gloomy even with the lights on. There were a number of portraits hung on the walls around the room and she went to study them one by one.

"Not a one of them seems happy!" Steve observed, looking over her shoulder. He had the urge to place his hands on her silk clad shoulders, to bend his mouth to her beautiful swan's neck and kiss it but he kept his hands and his mouth to himself.

"They do look a touch subdued," Meredith remarked. "You've inherited the family face."

"Meredith, I've heard that for years and years," he told her in a satirical voice.

"Well, it's a very handsome face. It could have been ugly."

"That wouldn't have worried me if I'd had a *name*."

She moved on to the portrait of a very fragile-looking lady in a white silk morning gown. "It was all very sad, Steven, but you've been acknowledged now."

"Yes, indeed!" he agreed dryly. "My new status has certainly made a huge difference to your mother and father. Let's get a glass of something."

"I wouldn't mind a glass of wine," Meredith said, all her nerves jumping. She knew she couldn't count on herself not to surrender to anything he wanted. Indeed, she felt her entire tingling body belonged to him. Wasn't that proof perfect she loved him? "I don't expect there's a wine cellar."

"This isn't Coronation Hill, Ms McKendrick," he pointed out suavely.

"There might be, you never know." She sounded hopeful. "Let's take a good look upstairs before we go in search of one. I want to take this dress off anyway. It's depressing me. Sarah left me a couple of things to tide me over until I go home *tomorrow*," she stressed. "We're pretty much of a size."

His glance swept her. It held so much heat it sizzled her to the bone. "Sarah's actually thin," he said a little worriedly. Sarah was, indeed, too thin. "But you're very slender and lithe. You stand very straight. I like that. But I know what you mean. I'll change myself, then we can hunt up some food. The piles of sandwiches didn't take long to disappear and I had nothing."

"Neither did I."

"Nevertheless funerals evidently make a lot of other people hungry."

"And thirsty," Meredith added, thinking it hadn't just been tea and coffee that had quickly been downed. Whiskey decanters had been drained.

"I don't like this staircase," Steve said, not able to prevent himself from admiring her legs. High heels on a woman were infinitely sexy.

"Neither do I," she said, not about to let him in on the idea she had for relocating the staircase. She had her reasons for keeping him guessing. In fact, she had to confess to herself she was rather enjoying it, even on such a sombre day.

"So which bedroom do you want?" Steve asked, as they moved along the wide corridor.

Meredith spoke up so casually they might have been cousins. "I'll take Cate's. It's been aired and made up. Julie has been so good. She's quietly seen to a lot of things." She walked into the large old-fashioned bedroom that looked towards the front of the house. A verandah to walk out onto would have been perfect, but that would have to wait.

What am I thinking, for goodness sake! She was actually re-decorating the house in her head.

"What about you?" she asked airily, stepping back to admire the embroidered silk coverlet on the bed.

"I think I'll just head across the hall." He turned his crow-black head in that direction.

"To Sarah's room?"

"I don't want to get *too* far away," he told her with a mocking smile. "You're not mentioning you're damned nervous, but I know you are."

"It's an unfamiliar house," she replied, defensively. "Moreover, one expects some kind of nervousness on such a day." In reality she was spooked.

He nodded, beginning to walk away. He might pretend to be at ease but all his senses were doing a slow burn. "All the signs augur for a thunderstorm during the night. If you're frightened you don't have to wait for an invitation to come over."

"Sorry, Steven," she called after him. "I come from the Territory, remember?"

He paused at the door, his face the face of the portraits downstairs. "It might shock you to learn, Ms McKendrick, the electrical storms here are even worse. Now, I'm going to change out of this undertaker gear. Knock on my door when you're ready to go in search of the wine cellar. Let's hope Julie has done us a service leaving us some food."

Left alone Meredith looked quickly at what Cate had left her. A pretty loose dress in an ink-blue and white pattern, a sort of trapeze dress with short ruffled sleeves and a double ruffle at the hem. That would do nicely, lovely and cool. There was a pair of navy flatties a half a size too big but she was glad of them. She rarely wore high heels; a pink cotton nightdress, pintucked and embroidered with tiny grub roses, matching robe, very virginal. Both sisters were easy to like. She saw how life might have been hard for them without their mother, and knowing they had a half brother somewhere they had been forbidden to meet.

Meredith went to the solid mahogany door and closed it, without actually turning the lock. Would she forget to lock it tonight?

"I'll be damned if this isn't the best room in the house," Steven was saying, his surprised glance sweeping the large cellar with its attractive rustic ambience. The ceiling was dark beamed, the walls stone, as was the floor with a wide stone archway dividing the wine storage area with its long rows of racks from a seating, dining area if needs be. There were two big leather armchairs in front of a fireplace obviously well used—the desert could grow very cold at night—and a long refectory table with eight Jacobean style chairs set around it. There was even a strikingly realistic rural oil painting of a herd of cattle fording a coolibah-lined creek.

"Someone spent a lot of time here," Meredith observed, hunting at the bottom of the canvas for the name of the artist.

"So what do we want?"

"White for me," Meredith said, shivering a little because the cellar was so much cooler than the house. "A sauvignon Blanc."

"A sauvignon Blanc it is." Steve picked a bottle up, passing it to her while he hunted up a Shiraz for himself. Maybe there was a steak or two in the fridge? Euroka was a cattle station after all.

No steaks, but a leg of ham, bacon, plenty of eggs, cream, milk, cheese, a basket full of bright red tomatoes, a brown paper bag full of mushrooms; and in the bread bin a loaf of sour dough bread, obviously freshly baked.

"Looks like ham and eggs," Meredith said. "We can pretend it's breakfast."

"Ah, to think we really *will* be having breakfast together." Steve said, mockery in his expression. But the emotion was there. "Look at you, a little housewife!" Meredith had tied a clean apron around her waist to protect Cate's dress.

"Do you think you can get away with this because we're on our own?" she asked, briefly lifting her eyes to him. He was wearing a red T-shirt with his jeans and he looked extraordinarily vivid, vibrating with a physical energy that was like a force field around him. It was very impressive.

"Get away with what exactly?" he asked, though he knew precisely what she meant. He was goading her. He didn't want to, but he was.

"Your resentments are evident, Steven," she said, but went no further. The atmosphere between them was inflammatory enough.

He shrugged. "You're better off with me than at home I'd say."

Meredith didn't acknowledge that, either. She took six large eggs out of their carton. "Shall I scramble them? There's plenty of cream."

"Are there no ends to your talents, Ms McKendrick?" He tipped out the mushrooms that needed a wipe over. "Scrambled will be fine. Why don't you have a glass of the red while you wait for your wine to chill?"

"I think I'd drink anything at the moment." She gave a faint sigh. The strain was telling on both of them. She began to break the eggs into a bowl adding the cream.

"I'll find us some glasses. *Nice* glasses." Steve hunted through the numerous cupboards before he hit the mother lode, crystal. He filled two glasses and put one beside Meredith's hand.

"Thank you." Meredith took a good sip of the wine. It was ruby-red and very good.

A sudden gust of wind blew strongly through the back door, pungent with bush incense. Steve went to close it. "I know we'll get rain," he said. "I just know it."

Lightning was a dazzling white illumination, searing the retinas of her eyes. Meredith hid her head beside a stack of pillows. She could have pulled the curtains but she had no desire whatever to sleep in the pitch-dark. The bedroom was oddly cold. Could she risk getting up and finding a blanket? Why not? Steven wasn't going to come to her. She had to bow low before him. The truth was he hadn't forgiven her for her apparent rejection.

You'd come if you loved me.

And if you don't, I'll disappear out of your life.

That had been the implication. What had she done? She'd waffled on about meeting up again in a little while. That had been a mistake. Now, apart from ensuring she had stayed with him, he was acting as cool as you please.

"Good night, Meredith!"

"Good night, Steven." She was far from happy, but she managed to sound as cool as he.

Both of them had been hungry, leaving not a morsel on their plates. There was ice-cream to follow; she found a tin of peaches. They finished the wine and then Steven made coffee. Afterwards they talked a good deal about running a big operation, something with which Meredith was well acquainted. She made a number of suggestions that he picked up on immediately, saying they were excellent and facetiously offering her a job. They talked about what would be expected of him, who might replace him on Jingoll, anything and everything except their personal relationship and where it was going, if anywhere. It was a huge jump from desire to consummation. She realised she wasn't going to be allowed to get away with that perceived humiliation.

Surely he realised she couldn't have turned her back on everyone and eloped with him on the spot? She had obligations. It would have taken her a little time to put her affairs in order, then pack her bags if that was what he wanted; not that she didn't understand where he was coming from. Steven had lacked real commitment from childhood. His family had virtually abandoned him by the time he reached adolescence. What a blow that must have been! What a heartache for a young boy! When he had suggested she go with him to Jingoll, a *yes* answer had been crucial. In some ultrasensitive corner of his mind she had failed him, even if he could rationalise the difficulties of her position.

Then there was her parents' embarrassing back flip. Who could blame him if he was contemptuous of that? Surely he couldn't think his change of fortune had had any influence on her? All her adult life she had kept herself very much under control. She had been waiting for the right moment to make her move. She had, in fact, been working steadily towards it when Fate stepped in.

Around three in the morning the rain advanced from the north like a large army on the march. Meredith heard it coming minutes before it actually arrived. Then when it did, the storm broke with ferocity, a driving deluge that changed direction within seconds as the wind chopped this way and that. Now it was pelting through the open casement windows, whipping up the curtains that went into a wild dance.

Meredith turned on a bedside light, then sprang out of bed, but by the time she got to the windows the rain was lashing the bedroom floor. Half blinded, she managed to get one window down without much trouble, apart from being drenched—indeed, the flimsy nightgown was almost ripped from her body—but the sash on the middle window abruptly broke as she was lowering it. It came crashing down with fragments of glass flying like steel chips.

Instantly she jumped back before the chips could stab her, curling up her bare toes against the broken glass that now lay on the floor.

"Meredith?"

It was Steven banging on the door, his voice charged with anxiety.

"It's open!"

He burst into the room, shirtless, his jeans pulled on in obvious haste, zipped but not buttoned. She could see the low line of his navy hipsters. "Don't move!" he ordered, taking in the situation at a glance.

"You've got bare feet, too," she warned him, rain all over her face and in her eyes.

He yanked up a cushion and swished it a few times over an area of the wet floor. Then he pitched it into a corner. One armed he lifted her away and carried her that way back into the centre of the room. "You're soaking wet."

"I *know*. So are you!" His black hair, his bronze skin and his upper body were glistening. Yet he felt warm, whereas she was chilled.

"Hang on, I'll get a few towels." He rushed to turn on the lights in the bathroom, but she went after him her wet nightgown draped to her body like a second skin.

A few seconds more and she was swaddled in a large bath towel while he took a smaller one to her hair. "You'd better get out of that nightgown."

"*Excuse me,* not while you're looking!" She spoke huskily from behind the towel he was so energetically wielding.

"Then I'll turn away."

He did, throwing down the towel and turning his wide bare back.

"What are we going to do about the rain pouring in?" she asked, pulling the nightgown over her head in a kind of frenzy. Her heart was beating much too fast. She knotted the pink towel around her like a sarong, feeling incredibly nervous but her whole body aroused.

"We'll have to pray the storm passes over quickly or the wind changes. Or I can rig up something. Can I turn around now."

"Yes." She had never been more conscious of her own skin.

"Actually I could see you in the mirror."

She found that so electrifying her whole body broke out in a fabulous flush of excitement.

"Only joking," he murmured, his fingers reaching out to tidy her tumbled hair.

"Then I'm not amused."

"Neither am I. I've never felt less like laughing in my life." His eyes dropped the length of her body, and as he did so, his handsome face picked up a sharp shadow. "Your foot is bleeding."

"Is it?" She hadn't been aware of any cut or sting.

"Let me take a look," he said with concern. "Sit on the chair."

"Aren't we're supposed to be fixing the window?" She knew where all this was going but she wasn't about to stop it even for a tornado.

"I'll fix it when the rain stops. Right now I want to take a look at your foot."

"I don't remember standing on any glass." How could she

when she was concentrated on him? The bright light cast a mosaic of glittering jet on his hair, the whorls on his chest, the dark gold of his face, the skin of his shoulders, his strong arms and his sculpted torso. Who could blame her for feeling such piercing desire?

"You must have." He balanced her narrow foot in the palm of his hand. "It's not bad, just a bit of blood." He reached around for a box of tissues that were sitting on the counter. "I'll hold it until the bleeding stops." He glanced up at her, glittering sparks in his eyes. "You know, your toes are as pretty as your hands."

It might have been the most thrilling compliment she had ever received because she was instantly on fire. "Not a lot of people know that." She spoke shakily, finding the sensation of her foot resting in his hand incredibly erotic. She could even hear her heart banging furiously above the wild orchestration of the storm. It seemed to her to be passing over the roof in a dipping rush before swinging away.

He lifted her foot higher and pressed his mouth to her high instep. Then he began to lick it, curling his tongue over her soft skin down to her toes.

"Steven!" A moan came from the back of her arched throat.

"God, you're beautiful!" He said it in such a tender voice she couldn't help it. She burst into tears.

"Meredith!" His expression so frankly sensual, changed to concern. "You're all right? You're okay?"

She let her head fall forwards onto his shoulder, her breathing deepening. "I've missed you. Oh, God, how I've missed you! I want you back."

"And I want *you* back." He rose from his haunches, gathering her close up against him. "Tell me you love me. I'll never let you go otherwise."

She sank against his marvellous lean body, letting his chest hair graze her cheek. The pleasure she felt at being back in his arms was tremendous. "That's all right! I'm happy here." She gave a voluptuous sigh, pierced through with love.

"But I want to take you back to bed. *My* bed." His eyes had turned very dark with emotion. "You can't stay here anyway."

She lifted her face to him, blue eyes overbright, her hair in riotous disarray. "You're saying you want to sleep with me?"

"That's not the worst of it. I'm *going to!*" His gaze travelled down over her smooth shoulders to the cleft between her breasts barely concealed as the pink towel kept dipping lower and lower. "Surely you're overdressed in that?" he asked huskily.

Yearning poured into her. She no longer felt the need to deny or repress it. "Can I keep it on while I ask you a question?"

"Fire away." He pulled her in very tight, trapping her within his arms. "Ask me anything."

It rippled out with laughter. "What are your intentions, Steven Lancaster?"

He spoke against her lips. "Devilish!" His palms were running down over her silky shoulders, her sides, his fingers playing very gently with the folds of the towel. "Surely you already know? I want you. I'll never stop wanting you. I want to marry you."

She could see so clearly how wonderful that would be. Overcome with emotion, she dropped her head, barely able to speak.

"Look at me." He cupped her chin.

Tremors were shooting through her. She could feel the heat rising from his skin. She caught his musky male scent, the evaporated rain, saw the little pearl drops that still clung to him. She leaned forwards and tongued a few off. They tasted like some powerful aphrodisiac putting her in a fever of want.

"Would you have come to me if all this hadn't happened?" he asked. "Or would you have lost your nerve?" It was a serious question demanding a truthful answer.

Her throat was suddenly crowded with words. Then they came tumbling out as though to withhold them any longer would choke her. "Never. I'm so sorry what happened that last time, Steven. I wanted you to understand so badly. I know you felt I failed you. No, don't say anything. You *did*. But I was planning all the while. You stamped your name on me. Body and soul. I swear, I was never going to let you go." Her nerves were fluttering badly. She lifted her arms to lock them around his neck. "*Please* believe me." She was frantic he would. "Nothing and no one would have stoppe—"

She got no further. The flow of words was as abruptly cut off as the drumming rain.

His mouth was over hers, covering it, his tongue opening it up fully to his exploration. He kept going and going, thoroughly aroused, kissing her, staggering her with the force of his passion. The towel fell away unheeded, falling in a soft pile at their feet. She strained against him, while he grappled with her satiny naked body, her breasts crushed against his bare chest. For a long moment he held her back from him, studying her body, his glance alone ravishing her. She rose on tiptoes. She had never thought it possible to feel like this. He lifted her as though she weighed no more than a feather pillow.

Naked he put her down on his bed, leaving his strong hands on her shoulders, revelling in her expression that was wild with longing. For *him!*

"From this day forward we're bound together," he said in triumph, desiring her so much his entire body throbbed. He wanted nothing more than to bury himself deeply within her feeling the clutch of her around him. He wanted to merge himself with her. All his wildest dreams, his hopes, his expectations, so seemingly impossible had come true. He had made a great discovery. Meredith was the love of his life.

Blissfully, she sank back into the pillows and shut her eyes.

When she opened them again, *her man,* her lover was bending over her, staring down at her with such a world of longing in his eyes her limbs turned liquid.

She cried out his name in an ecstasy of need. "Steven, my true love, come here to me."

He obeyed, awed by the realisation he was about to take this wonderful woman in a way he hitherto had only dreamed about.

CHAPTER NINE

LIFE was always dealing out surprises. Almost overnight Jocelyn had undergone a remarkable sea change. The histrionics disappeared. Previously unable and unwilling to conceal her dismay that things were not what she had hoped for, Jocelyn now set about making the best of things. Robbie had a lot to do with it, Gina thought. There was no doubt in anyone's mind Jocelyn really loved Robbie. He was a beautiful child, his father's son, of course, natural, easy, comforting and loving with his grandmother. That was the irony of it, Gina thought. If Cal had brought only Robbie and not her back to Coronation Hill, Jocelyn would have been over the moon. As it was, Jocelyn had discovered it wasn't pleasant being the odd man out. Ewan and Meredith had accepted her. In fact, one would have thought she was the girl Ewan had in mind for his son all along.

Even Steven Lancaster—the young man Ewan McKendrick had appeared to hate so much—was now very much in the picture. Meredith had come home from the Lancaster stronghold, so happy, so radiant, so obviously very much in love, her imminent engagement to Steven was received with exclamations of congratulations and every appearance of pleasure. Even Jocelyn knew better than to risk a sarcastic comment.

"Marvellous, isn't it?" Meredith commented later to her brother. "It seems I've done something right at long last!"

Gina found Robbie in one of his favourite places, the beautiful Garden Room, Jocelyn always called the Conservatory. He was sitting at a small circular table flanked by Rosa and Uncle Ed who had taken over elements of his education. A big picture book was open in front of him, his glossy, dark head bent over it. Rosa saw Gina first.

"So where are you off to, *cara?*" Her brilliant dark eyes swept over Gina. She was in riding costume, which pretty well answered the question. It really suited her Rosa saw with pride and pleasure. Her Gina had a beautiful body. She wasn't so sure about Jocelyn McKendrick as a teacher for her beloved godchild. But it appeared Jocelyn had been a fine rider in her day and still rode, though not as frequently. She had offered to give Gina riding lessons on the quiet. It was to be a big surprise for Cal.

"Mummy, Mummy," Robbie broke in excitedly, "Uncle Ed found a book for me all about the planets. Do you know what the word *planet* means?"

Gina went to him and kissed his warm rosy cheek. "No, my darling, I don't. Please tell me."

"It means *wanderer* because the planets wander across the sky."

"Well, that's what the ancient Greeks *thought,* Robbie," Ed told him. "In fact, the planets all circle the Sun. They move in the same direction, in much the same plane and each spins on its axis as it orbits." He demonstrated with a finger and a twirling movement of his hand. "You have a very bright boy here, Gina." Ed looked up to smile at her. "He just soaks up knowledge. It's a pleasure for Rosa and me to have anything to do with his education."

Rosa reached out and covered Ed's hand with her own.

They'll probably beat Cal and me down the aisle, Gina thought as she moved off. But they'd have to be awfully quick. The wedding invitations had been sent out. It was to be a small wedding. No more than fifty people. Neither of them wanted a big affair. Each night he came to her. Lying beside her on the bed until she finally went off to sleep, her body wanting nothing more after the tumultuous passion they aroused in each other. Their sex life was glorious. It could hardly have been bettered, but their trust in each other lagged behind. The lost years, the old grieves, the needless suffering, needed time to be erased, before each had full confidence in the other. Both of them desperately required forgiveness of themselves and one another.

They had decided for Robbie's sake they wouldn't openly share a bedroom until after the wedding. Gina couldn't wait. They had talked about a honeymoon. They didn't want to leave Robbie. The love between father and son had developed at a tremendous rate. That was Cal's big problem with her, Gina thought sadly. She had deprived him of his son for three of the most precious years of life. Cal had taken that greatly to heart. She was terrified that deprival might in time be forgiven but never forgotten. What Cal required of her from now on, was her total allegiance.

She arrived at the stables complex a minute or so late. It was set amidst beautiful trees, with a training yard, almost a small track, enclosed by a high white painted picket fence facing it. Jocelyn, looking very trim and youthful, was waiting for her in the cobbled courtyard. Their horses had been saddled up by one of the stable boys—and there appeared to be quite a number. Gina's mount was a pretty liver-chestnut mare called Arrola—which meant *beautiful* in aboriginal—with a star on its forehead and four white sox.

"Just the horse for a novice like you," Jocelyn had decided briskly.

Arrola, who really did have a lovely nature, extended its velvety muzzle to be stroked. Gina made an affectionate, low clicking sound she had learned from Jocelyn that appeared to work. That first time she had prayed she would stay on. She was still praying after half a dozen lessons, but she had settled a good deal. She had to admit Jocelyn was an excellent teacher, very patient, showing no sign of disappointment or disapproval when Gina couldn't perform as expected. Gina had come to the conclusion—and she was being very hard on herself—she wasn't a natural as all the McKendricks were and Robbie would prove to be, but she was quickly gaining an acceptable level of expertise. Jocelyn wouldn't tolerate less.

Jocelyn always chose the route they would take, always away from where the men would be working. This was to be a surprise for Cal after all. The two of them always rode alongside, Jocelyn constantly offering instruction on some aspect of posture and handling of the reins. Today was a new route along a chain of billabongs densely wooded around the banks. The onset of the monsoon season had brought in a few storms but the earth beneath them was hard, giving Gina a feeling of security and solid leverage. Her leg and thigh muscles didn't ache half as much as they used to, either.

After twenty minutes or so, Jocelyn gave the order to quicken the pace. Ahead of them the giant landscape glimmered in the heat. The fragrance of wildflowers tossed up by the storms carried on the wind. In the distance, glittering through the thick screen of trees, some of them covered with scarlet flowers, were the billabongs alive with native birds and maybe the odd crocodile.

Gina, feeling a rush of excitement, lightly kicked Arrola's

flanks. She was beginning to appreciate how enormously exhilarating a gallop could be.

Riding up from the stream, Cal heard the drumbeats of hooves before he actually sighted the riders. Then as he cleared the trees a single rider burst into view, billows of dust rising as the rider's horse galloped out of control. A second rider came hot in pursuit; an expert this time. He recognised his mother's small frame.

"God!" he shouted, scarcely able to believe his eyes. Here was a tragedy waiting to happen. Galvanised, he swung into action, squeezing his big bay gelding's sides hard, urging it up the bank, then into a gallop. It couldn't be, it shouldn't be, but it was happening. That was Gina out there and she was in terrible danger. It struck him with tremendous force the devastation he would experience if she were injured. Or worse. He could see she had lost her hat, her long hair streaming on the wind. He recognised the horse. It was the little mare, Arrola, normally such a mild animal. Now it was clearly in a mad panic, galloping wildly towards the line of trees with Gina clinging desperately to its back. Her stirrups appeared to be lost. If she got flung off—and God knows how she was staying on—she would come down in a fearful mass of broken bones. If she managed to stay on, the mare would only continue its crazed gallop on to the trees. There she would have no hope. She would plough into a tree-trunk, or be hit by a large branch, her neck broken, her limbs snapped.

His heart froze. Why had he held back on telling her how much he loved her? he flayed himself. Why had he continued to blame her for not contacting him when she found herself pregnant? He had the right to know, sure, but why had he wanted to keep punishing her? Maybe she had kept a momentous event secret from him, but she must have suffered carrying their child alone. He had wasted so much time nursing his hurts, instead of trying to let them go. Even when he found out Lorinda and his mother had plotted against them, he had still kept on blaming Gina. She should have come to him. He could have put things straight. She hadn't trusted him. The grievances had gone on and on.

Now *this?*

There suddenly existed, right out of the blue, the dreadful possibility he might never get to tell her how much he loved her. How desperately he wanted her There had not been enough talk about matters of the heart. He had laboured to hide his very real love for her and he had to bitterly regret that. She could go to her death not knowing. That was unimaginable. No way could he let it happen.

His mother's horse, Dunbar, was a splendid animal. It never stumbled. It was eating up the ground but he realised it would never overtake the little mare. The mare must have had a considerable lead he calculated, his heart twisting in pain at the fleeting thought his mother could have been in some way responsible. Even as the thought came into his mind, he rejected it absolutely. His mother had her faults but she would never do anything to harm anyone. Even her efforts to break up his island romance didn't come under the heading of a malicious act. She and Lorinda would have truly believed, however mistakenly, they were doing the right thing.

He rode like he had never ridden before, his face blanched with fear and a boiling dread. If there was a God in Heaven, He couldn't do this to him. To have refound the woman he loved only to lose her to a violent death? How could he survive such a tragedy without undergoing some tremendous alteration in his character?

He galloped on. A lesser horseman would never have closed in on the runaway so fast. The gelding was wondrously sure-footed in the rough. It didn't have the speed and power of his favourite stallion, but it was responding magnificently. They were coming at the runaway from an angle, cross country, whereas his mother was pounding straight after them. His mother, too, was in mortal danger, but still she kept going. She would have to get Dunbar under control soon, or she, too, ran the risk of getting pulped amid the wilderness of trees.

A final powerful surge and he was pulling the big gelding alongside. Immediately it and the little mare began to jostle for supremacy, the tall gelding easily winning out. On Gina's beautiful face was exhaustion and despair. "Hang in there, Gina!" Cal shouted, finely judging the precise moment to lunge after her reins.

Please, God, don't fail me!

The first line of trees, brilliant with flower loomed up.

His nerve held iron-hard.

Got them!

Now it was a ferocious battle to control two horses. He reined back hard. The gelding responded, the mare just wanted to keep on going as if it had a death wish. Superb horseman that he was Cal had to fight against being pulled from the saddle. Again he yanked back. The little mare was still putting up a mighty fight, hell-bent on hurling herself and her rider into the trees.

He gave her a bit of head, and then pulled back as violently as he dared without bringing them all down. "Whoa, now, easy, easy, easy…"

With the compliance of the gelding, so responsive to his every demand, he got the mare under some sort of control. "Easy, girl, easy!" The mare began to centre herself.

The thicket was no more than twenty-five yards away.

Gina fell into his arms, collapsing against him, burying her face against his chest. His strong arms encircled her as though he would never let her go. All his defences, all his efforts to keep his real feelings in check were swept away.

His mother rode up, her face paper white. "My God, Cal," she gasped, chest heaving. "Only *you* could have done it. Gina could have lost her life." She spoke with the tremendous relief of a person who had seen a horror averted.

One arm still strongly around Gina, Cal went to his mother's assistance helping her dismount. There were tears coursing down her face. "My fault, my fault," she kept saying. "I'm so sorry, son. We wanted it to be a big surprise for you."

"Whatever happened?" His mother looked too distraught to really question, but he had to know at least that. Gina was in shock. She was very pale and trembling. So far she hadn't spoken a word.

"A bloody kangaroo!" His mother who rarely swore, swore with gusto. Anything to relieve her pent-up feelings. "Gina has been doing so well I thought we could try a little gallop. All would have been well, only the 'roo just popped up in front of her, spooking that silly mare. Spooked good old Dunbar, too, for that matter. He did quite a dance. If Gina had had more experience she could have reined the mare in. Instead Arrola took off as though she was going for the post in the Melbourne Cup. I didn't know she had it in her. I'm so dreadfully, dreadfully sorry. I would never have forgiven myself if anything had happened to Gina." Jocelyn looked into her son's eyes, frightened.

"I know that, Mum," he said gently.

At his response Jocelyn rallied. "Well, we'd better get her home," she said, already swinging herself back into the saddle. "A shot of brandy should do it. Some good strong black coffee. Always helped me. I'll ride ahead. Get one of the men to bring the Jeep. Bear up, Gina, girl," she called down to Gina in such a bracing voice Gina might just have been blooded. "It's a miracle you managed to stay on. I can think of any number who would have fallen off."

Jocelyn kicked her sweating horse into a gallop, determined

to outrun her lapse of judgement. The girl had guts. Damned if she didn't!

Gina remained within the half circle of Cal's arm, dragging in fortifying breaths. She was very pale but he thought it unlikely at this stage she would go into a faint.

"This is just a suggestion," he murmured quietly. "I could take you up before me on the gelding. You would be quite safe and we'd meet up with the Jeep quicker. If you prefer not to, shake your head."

His tone was so gentle and comforting Gina nodded her head. "Okay!"

"Okay what, Gina?" His expression relaxed a little.

"I'll ride with you." She turned up a face that showed a mixture of trepidation and bravery.

"I'll never let you come to harm," he said, making no effort to hide his depth of feeling. "Just trust me."

"I do," she whispered. She had the sense many of the defences he had put up against her had toppled.

"I really don't deserve it." His brief laugh was ragged.

"You saved my life. Whatever would have happened to me if you hadn't turned up?"

"Don't even think about it." Cal shuddered.

"Death by freak accident."

"Hush!" Of course, it happened. Freak accidents weren't uncommon in station life.

"It was all for you, the riding," Gina wanted to reassure him. "Your mother had faith in me. I let her down."

"God, no," Cal protested violently, greatly upset even if he appeared in control. "The best station horses can be spooked. Horses are such nervous animals and the 'roos have a bad habit of popping up out of nowhere. You'll learn how to keep a horse under control."

"Is that why you want me to get on one again!" She gave a ghost of a laugh.

"Not today if you don't want to." His arm tightened around her. It was a relief to hear her voice strengthening and see colour coming back into her cheeks.

"Then I have to tell you the only one I'd do it for is *you!*"

Back at the homestead Gina found herself being fussed over.

"You can go off now, Cal," Jocelyn said after about an hour and several cups of tea later. "Gina will be fine now. We'll look after her, won't we, Robbie, darling?"

"We'll spoil her!" Robbie stoutly maintained.

Cal stood up, looked down at Gina, reclining on the sofa. "I'll stay if you want me to." God, he'd do *anything* she wanted.

"That's okay, I know you've got lots to do. I'm fine. Really!" In fact, she had never felt so safe and sound.

"We'll look after her, Daddy." Robbie gazed up at his father. "Won't we, Nan?" Robbie had taken to calling Jocelyn Nan of his own accord. "It bothers you, doesn't it, Daddy, Mummy got such a fright?"

Cal smiled down on his very perceptive little son. "You can say that again, pal!"

"Mummy's brave all the time," Robbie announced proudly.

At that moment, Rosa, who had been taking a leisurely drive with Edward, rushed in, closely followed up by a concerned-looking Edward, their gazes falling on Gina. "What is this I hear?" Rosa asked worriedly.

Gina thought it time to move. She swung her feet determinedly to the floor. "No fuss, Rosa, dear. I'm fine."

"You look upset?" Rosa's dark eyes flashed accusingly around the room, focusing on Jocelyn. Her baby needed protection.

"Mummy doesn't want to talk about it, Rosa, okay?" Robbie

jogged over to Rosa and took her hand in his. "She got a fright when her horse bolted, but Daddy saved her from any danger. No one is as good as my daddy. He's a marvellous rider. Now we're helping Mummy get over it. Would you and Uncle Edward like a cup of tea?"

Rosa blinked and caught her breath. "Coffee, I think, sweetheart," she said. "I must admit I panicked."

Jocelyn stood up immediately, all graciousness. "I'll go organise a pot. It won't be too long before it's ready."

For the rest of the day Gina took it quietly, but by evening she was over the worst of her shock. She was alive when she could have been a serious casualty. Or dead. Everyone appeared enormously grateful. For the first time there was genuine accord around the table, Jocelyn leaning over to touch Gina's hand several times during the meal. Even Ewan put his hand on top of Gina's and gave it a little squeeze. Gina didn't realise it but everyone thought she was standing up to a very frightening incident awfully well. Meredith, who had been staying with Steven for a couple of days working out how best to refurbish Euroka's homestead, had been startled and upset by the news when she phoned in earlier in the evening.

"It must have given you a tremendous fright, Gina," she said. "And Mum, too. When I spoke to her she was trying hard not to cry. What a miracle Cal was around to save you. You'll have to make it up to him tonight, girl!" This she proffered with a smile in her voice.

The very least I can do! Gina felt a rush of affection for her soon to be sister-in-law.

The household settled around eleven o'clock and a short time later Cal tapped on her bedroom door.

He stood looking down at her, a bottle of champagne and two

flutes in hand, a white linen napkin draped over his arm. "Room service, madam."

"Please come in," she said, as though he were exactly that, but her whole body was instantly a-pulse.

"Sometimes nothing else will do but champagne," he offered smoothly.

"It certainly helps." Gina turned and saw them both reflected in the mirror of the dressing table; he with his impressive height, densely, darkly, vividly masculine; she with her flowing hair and glowing skin, dressed only in a satin robe, the quintessential image of alluring woman. As an image it appeared incredibly erotic. "Do we have something to celebrate?" Her dark eyes watched him.

"You know we have. This has been quite a day." He leaned to graze her cheek. "There *is* a God," he announced.

"Of course there is." Gina moved to take up a position on the invitingly cosy chaise longue covered in a lovely pale green silk. "I've never doubted it."

"And I never will again!" Cal said, his voice filled with real gravity. He didn't think the memory of the immense blessing they had been granted that afternoon would ever leave him. Gently, he twisted the cork from the bottle, muffling the loud *pop* with the linen napkin. "I should have brought a wine cooler," he said, partially filling one flute then the other. "You do realise the silk on the couch is the same colour as your robe?"

"That's why I'm sitting here," she said, her voice silken cool. Gracefully she accepted her flute from him, deliriously close to swooning. "Sit beside me. There's plenty of room." She patted the smooth surface.

He gave her his achingly beautiful smile. "The damn thing is almost as wide as a double bed. We might try it here one night." Emerald eyes glittered as he moved slowly towards her. "To us!"

His breath ended on a faint groan. "For gut-pulverising moments this afternoon I thought I was going to lose you."

They clinked glasses, their eyes locking. "You do want me around then?"

He continued to soak her in. "How can you say that?"

She pushed back the long cuffed sleeve of her robe. "You've been very…conflicted, Cal. You can't deny it. I could tell."

He smarted inside, knowing the charge was right. "Tonight is going to be different," he promised, low voiced. "You tore the heart from me, Gina. Afterwards…" He paused, shrugged a shoulder, then settled opposite her on the chaise. "Some things you can't help."

"I know. I've gained a lot of experience these past few years. It wasn't supposed to happen like it happened," she said with profound regret. "I should have done something."

"*I* should have done something." The admission continued his liberation. "Think how different it would have been." He captured her free hand, studying her pearly fingernails, inflamed to be near her. "I should have married you four years ago. I had the wisdom to fall in love with you. I lacked the wisdom to see through Lorinda. She was enormously convincing and she was family. I believed she loved me and had my best interests at heart."

"And so she did by her lights." Gina spoke with intensity. "That's what made the deception so easy. You trusted her because she was family. I trusted her because I truly believed I wasn't good enough for you."

His hand pulled away. "Is that what she said?" he asked sharply, his face tautened into an angry mask.

Gina glanced straight head. A fresh arrangement of exquisite tropical orchids had been placed on the nearby table. "I believed it," she repeated, thinking it wasn't a good thing to store up the mistakes of the past. Life wasn't long enough to hold on to thoughts of vengeance.

"And what do you believe now?" he demanded, swiftly draining his glass, then setting it down.

She hesitated a moment. "*You* mightn't be good enough for *me!*"

He laughed aloud, charmed and amused by the little expression of hauteur. "Drink up," he ordered. "I'm going to make love to you far into the night."

"Really?" She exhaled voluptuously, unable to hide her sensual pleasure. "That will be wonderful! But I need more from you than desire, Cal McKendrick, however ravishing."

"Desire is only part of it, *Gianina,*" he assured her. Those moments of terror when he had thought she could be killed, had clearly shown him his own heart. He loved her so much he wanted to go down on his knees before her.

"Then tell me about the other part," she invited, holding her empty flute for a refill.

He stood up. "You have a mind to make me wait?" He glanced back over his shoulder, seeing more of her golden flesh exposed as the robe slid off her ravishingly sexy long legs.

Gina's smile was slow. "It's more that I want these moments to last. You delight and astonish me with your lovemaking, Cal, but you have never said *I love you.*"

He rejoined her on the couch, handing back her glass. "Surely that applies to us both? I've never heard it from you. At least, of recent times."

She tongued a bead of champagne around the rim of the flute into her mouth. Delicious! "Too much confusion. Too much pain. I thought the love you once had for me—or I thought you once had for me—had disappeared."

He leaned forwards to brush his mouth over hers, tasting the delicate yet intense fruity flavours on her luscious lips. He would never, never, never find another woman like Gina. "Where could the love go?" he asked. "It was always there. All locked up inside me." He drew his head back, murmuring, "You really do look like a goddess."

His desiring gaze enveloped her in flame. "A goddess?" She laughed shakily. "Not at all. I'm just a woman."

"If you were only *just* a woman I might have found it easier to forget you." When he spoke again his voice was edged with agitation. "I never got to be with you when our son was born."

She quickly set down her glass; cradled his beloved dark head. "And how I missed you! I cried out your name, not once but many times. Everyone in that delivery room knew the first name of my child's father if they were not to know the last."

He drew back, staring into her huge velvety eyes, brilliant with the glaze of tears. "I should have been there." His voice carried a mixture of great conviction and pain.

"You'll be there next time," she whispered, afraid she was going to break down.

"I couldn't forget you, Gina." His voice cracked with strong emotion.

"No more than I could forget you." She tried to encircle him with her arms, leaning into him to kiss his mouth. "Do you believe in Destiny?"

"I do now!" Cal's hands moved to her shoulders, peeling back her robe, then he dropped to his knees in front of her, his open mouth brushing against her throat, moving down lingeringly to the fragrant slopes of her full breasts. His strong hands were drawing her in nearer and nearer. Finally he eased the robe off her naked body cradling her back with his spread hand. "You're mine and I'm yours!"

Womanlike, she teased him, shaking her tumbled head. "I want you to prove it."

He didn't answer. He only smiled, picking her up and carrying her to the huge four-poster bed where he laid her down and slowly began to practise his magic on her.

"I truly, truly love you," he softly whispered.

"I truly, truly, love you."

"And I will to my last breath."

That night they made love not only with their bodies, but to the depths of their souls.

Days later Cal announced he was going to fly a blissfully happy Gina to Broome to buy her some pearls. "My wedding present to her. We'll only be gone a day or two."

Immediately Robbie piped up. "Can I come, too, Daddy?"

Cal placed his hand gently on his son's head. "Not this time, Robert, but I'll have a big surprise for you when we get home."

Robbie caught his mother's eye. "What *is* it?" he asked in a loud stage whisper.

"A surprise is a surprise, my darling," she told him, her mind already on giving him a little brother or sister to love. "But you're going to absolutely *love* it!" she promised.

Robbie gazed back at her steadily for a moment then he cried out in an ecstasy of excitement. "It's the pony!"

"Careful now, Robbie, you'll tip over your chair." Ewan reached out to steady it, looked at the child fondly. What a great little chap he was! Of course it was the pony. Every McKendrick had his own pony by Robert's age.

"Don't worry about Robbie, you two," Jocelyn said, flashing her grandson a big conspiratorial smile. "He'll be fine with me!" She couldn't help but hope at her rival for Robbie's affections the flamboyant Rosa would soon move off and take the besotted Ed with her. "I adore pearls as you all know. They'll suit you beautifully, Gina, with your lovely skin. Our South Sea Pearls are recognised all over the world as the finest of all white pearls. 'The Queen of Gems' they're called."

The multi-cultural city of Broome, with a vast red desert behind it and the azure-blue Indian Ocean in front of it, was a fascinating melting pot of nationalities Gina found. European, Chinese, Japanese, Malay, Koepanger and Aboriginal cultures were all represented. Broome had quite a history going back to its founding as a pearling port. It was the English seaman and pirate, William Dampier who was credited with having discovered Western Australia's fabulous Kimberley region for which Broome was the port. That was way back in 1688, when Dampier first visited "New Holland" bringing Britain's attention to the area's rich pearl shell beds.

Gina actually owned little jewellery outside the costume variety so the afternoon's shopping expedition was very exciting, especially when the sky seemed to be the limit. The pearls that were put on display for them took her breath away. At first she didn't know what size she should be looking at. Even strands of smallish pearls were worth thousands. The boutique assistant steered them towards another showcase.

More strands were laid out for her. They were all so beautiful she stood staring down at them not sure what she should pick. No price was being mentioned. The assistant must have taken her silence for some tiny sign of dissatisfaction because she turned away and came back with a shorter strand, a *necklet* of magnificent, large pearls.

"That's it!" Cal proclaimed immediately. "That's what we want. You should have shown us these first," he said, softening the remark with one of his smiles. "Turn around darling so I can put them on. We'll need earrings to match. Pendant earrings, maybe a little channel of diamonds above the pearl?"

The assistant returned the smile warmly. It was a long time since she had seen such a *gorgeous* couple. And they were so very much in love! She loved it when couples like that came in.

It was the grandest day, full of happiness and excitement and the day wasn't over.

Gina was finishing dressing for dinner—they had taken a suite—when Cal entered the bedroom. "I have someone in the sitting room I'm sure you'll want to meet," he announced casually.

She looked up quickly. That peculiar little tingle had started up at her nape. It didn't simply touch her, either. It actually began to *tap* away. "Okay. Do I look all right?" She presented herself for his inspection. She was wearing a new silk halter dress, very sophisticated, with a plunging neckline. Too plunging?

Cal didn't look like he minded. In fact, his eyes glittered with pure desire. "Yes, yes and *yes!*" he exclaimed, bending to kiss her on her luscious mouth. "But you must come along now."

"Who is it?" Her voice had turned quavery. "Or aren't I allowed to ask?"

"Oh, it's someone you know." He gave her a reassuring smile.

The tapping grew stronger.

"Are you going to ask them to join us at dinner?" Was it a man, or a woman? she briefly speculated.

A man, the voice inside her head said.

She felt like she was travelling on some new stretch of road. Cal took her trembling hand in his, drawing her into the sitting room. "Gina, my darling, he might have been a very hard man to find but I'm sure you're happy to see him!"

Shock and triumph folded into one another. Gina stood speechless for a moment then she cried: *"Sandro!"* It was a cry that came from the depths of her heart. "*My* Sandro! Oh, Cal, will I *ever* be able to thank you? This is wonderful, wonderful!" One brilliant upwards glance at the man soon to be her husband, then Gina rushed towards her long lost brother who stood there with tears unashamedly coursing down his sculpted cheeks.

"How could you? How could you, Sandro?" Gina beat her fists against her brother's chest. "There's not a day I haven't missed you!"

"Forgive me," he begged. "I have so missed you, but I never knew Papa was dead. You know with him alive I could never go back."

"Well, you're not going to leave us again." Gina shook a warning head. "I won't let you."

Sandro, dark and handsome, perfectly beautiful to his sister's eyes, opened his arms wide.

Cal stood back watching with satisfaction their highly emotional reunion. He felt justifiably pleased with himself. "Back in fifteen minutes," he announced, moving smoothly to the door. Brother and sister could do with some time together before they all went down to dinner.

His determination to find Gina's brother had paid off. It had taken weeks for his agents to find him, finally tracking him to Broome, of all places. Sandro had changed his name without going to a whole lot of bother. He was now Alec Sanders, a valued employee of the largest pearling outfit in the region.

Nothing is going to part those two again, Cal thought, happy to bring Gina's Sandro into the family. Broome, after all, was on their doorstep. From now on they all were to look to the future.

EPILOGUE

The McKendrick-Romano Wedding
Zoe Caldwell
Aurora Magazine.

I DO, I do, I do!
You all know the words! But do you know just how much excitement a girl can cram into a week-end? I'll tell you, a thrill a minute. Not the end of story. There was hardly a dry eye at the fabulous McKendrick pad, a vast cattle station in the Northern Territory, after the most moving wedding ceremony held in a flower-decked folly erected in the extravagantly beautiful tropical grounds of the homestead where this lucky social editor was privileged to stay. These cattle barons sure know how to live! Bride and groom had opted for a small private affair (not the rumoured *huge* affair coming up for the McKendrick heiress, Meredith, in a couple of months' time) but all the more intimate because of that. The bride looked a goddess come down to earth in a strapless white sheath dress with gold detailing, and an exquisite gold headdress. A fortune in pearls adorned her neck and swung from her earlobes. She was attended by her matron of honour, Mrs Tanya Fielding, in a divine, strapless, yellow silk chiffon gown, and her sister-in-law, Meredith McKendrick,

breathtaking in a matching strapless gown of a wonderful, harmonising shade of iris blue. Last but not least, there was the little page boy, the couple's adorable three-year-old son, Master Robert McKendrick who behaved perfectly throughout, or all the time I had my eye on him anyway! The bridegroom was attended by best man, Ross Sunderland, of North Star Station, another trillion square miles Territory spread, and his soon to be brother-in-law, Steven Lancaster, of the Queensland Channel Country's Euroka Station. Quite a turnout of the dashing cattle barons! The bride was given away by her stunningly handsome brother. The bride's mother, Lucia—boy, the stars were in attendance when they handed out *that* family's looks!—and Dutch born stepfather, Kort Walstrum, travelled from their coffee plantation in New Guinea to join in the celebrations, confessing themselves thrilled to be there.

The McKendricks will honeymoon in Dubai, returning through Hong Kong and Bangkok. It's understood the McKendricks Senior, now their son and heir is married, will be spending a lot of time at their luxury Sydney Harbour front apartment, with frequent visits to the legendary station. A little birdie whistled in my ear we're not looking at two McKendrick weddings, but *three!* Mr Edward McKendrick, the bridegroom's uncle, is said to be planning to marry the bride's glamorous godmother, Rosa Gambaro!

So get up to the Territory, girls, if you're looking for romance. It's contagious! Hire a Lear jet if you have to! I can't remember the last time I had so much fun!

HARLEQUIN *Romance*

MEDITERRANEAN DADS

In the first of this emotional Mediterranean Dads duet,
nanny Julie is whisked away to a palatial Italian villa,
but she feels completely out of place in Massimo's
glamorous world. Her biggest challenge, though, is
ignoring her attraction to the brooding tycoon.

Look for

The Italian Tycoon
and the Nanny
by Rebecca Winters

in March wherever you buy books.

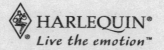

HARLEQUIN®
Live the emotion™

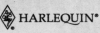

REQUEST YOUR FREE BOOKS!
2 FREE NOVELS PLUS 2
FREE GIFTS!

HARLEQUIN ROMANCE®

From the Heart, For the Heart

YES! Please send me 2 FREE Harlequin Romance® novels and my 2 FREE gifts. After receiving them, if I don't wish to receive any more books, I can return the shipping statement marked "cancel." If I don't cancel, I will receive 4 brand-new novels every month and be billed just $3.57 per book in the U.S., or $4.05 per book in Canada, plus 25¢ shipping and handling per book and applicable taxes, if any*. That's a savings of over 15% off the cover price! I understand that accepting the 2 free books and gifts places me under no obligation to buy anything. I can always return a shipment and cancel at any time. Even if I never buy another book from Harlequin, the two free books and gifts are mine to keep forever.

114 HDN EEV7   314 HDN EEWK

Name	(PLEASE PRINT)	
Address		Apt.
City	State/Prov.	Zip/Postal Code

Signature (if under 18, a parent or guardian must sign)

Mail to the **Harlequin Reader Service®:**
IN U.S.A.: P.O. Box 1867, Buffalo, NY 14240-1867
IN CANADA: P.O. Box 609, Fort Erie, Ontario L2A 5X3

Not valid to current Harlequin Romance subscribers.

Want to try two free books from another line?
Call 1-800-873-8635 or visit www.morefreebooks.com.

* Terms and prices subject to change without notice. NY residents add applicable sales tax. Canadian residents will be charged applicable provincial taxes and GST. This offer is limited to one order per household. All orders subject to approval. Credit or debit balances in a customer's account(s) may be offset by any other outstanding balance owed by or to the customer. Please allow 4 to 6 weeks for delivery.

Your Privacy: Harlequin is committed to protecting your privacy. Our Privacy Policy is available online at www.eHarlequin.com or upon request from the Reader Service. From time to time we make our lists of customers available to reputable firms who may have a product or service of interest to you. If you would prefer we not share your name and address, please check here. ☐

HR07

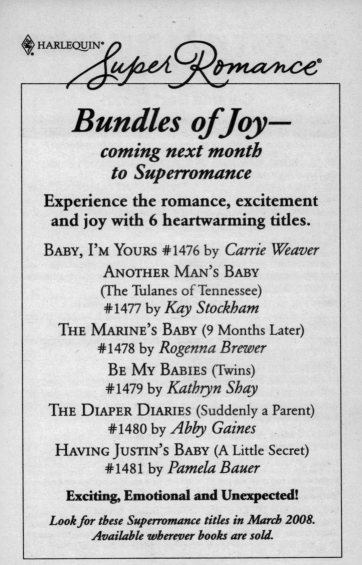

HARLEQUIN®

Super Romance®

Bundles of Joy—
coming next month to Superromance

Experience the romance, excitement and joy with 6 heartwarming titles.

BABY, I'M YOURS #1476 by *Carrie Weaver*

ANOTHER MAN'S BABY
(The Tulanes of Tennessee)
#1477 by *Kay Stockham*

THE MARINE'S BABY (9 Months Later)
#1478 by *Rogenna Brewer*

BE MY BABIES (Twins)
#1479 by *Kathryn Shay*

THE DIAPER DIARIES (Suddenly a Parent)
#1480 by *Abby Gaines*

HAVING JUSTIN'S BABY (A Little Secret)
#1481 by *Pamela Bauer*

Exciting, Emotional and Unexpected!

Look for these Superromance titles in March 2008.
Available wherever books are sold.

HARLEQUIN *Romance*

Coming Next Month

Join Harlequin Romance® in the fairy-tale mountains of Europe, on the shimmering Italian coast, at a grand Australian estate— and don't be late for an engagement in the boardroom!

#4009 A ROYAL MARRIAGE OF CONVENIENCE Marion Lennox
By Royal Appointment
Life doesn't always turn out the way you plan, right? As heir to the throne, Nikolai knows duty must always come first. But country vet Rose, his convenient wife-to-be, is not quite what Nikolai was expecting....

#4010 THE ITALIAN TYCOON AND THE NANNY Rebecca Winters
Mediterranean Dads
In the first book of this emotional duet, nanny Julie is whisked away to a palatial Italian villa, but feels completely out of place in Massimo's glamorous world. Her biggest challenge, though, is ignoring her attraction to the brooding tycoon....

#4011 PROMOTED: TO WIFE AND MOTHER Jessica Hart
Perdita's efficient, no-nonsense attitude works just fine in the boardroom. But when she meets executive Ed, and their business relationship becomes personal, she's left wondering whether being a wife and mother would suit her better.

#4012 FALLING FOR THE REBEL HEIR Ally Blake
It's definitely true that opposites attract, and Kendall couldn't be more different from Hudson Bennington III. She likes safe and secure—and he's got danger written all over him! But then he proposes a deal, and Kendall's tempted to accept....

#4013 TO LOVE AND TO CHERISH Jennie Adams
Heart to Heart
Sometimes we think we're better off coping with hardship alone, trying to protect the ones we love. When Jack went away he broke Tiffany's heart, but now that his demons are behind him, he's back—and determined to make things right.

#4014 THE SOLDIER'S HOMECOMING Donna Alward
Shannyn's beautiful daughter is a daily reminder of her true love, Jonas, who left town to be a soldier. Now that Jonas is back, hardened by war, Shannyn must find a way to reach his soul again for the sake of her daughter and the family she longs for.

HRCNM0208